A COMEDY SCI-FI ADVENTURE SERIES
BY

...Don't you have to be on board a ship to commit mutiny?...

BOOK THREE - PART THREE

ISBN 978-1-7398855-5-7

Paperback Version

DOWNFALL: PART THREE BY SAM LUCAS © 2022

WWW.SAMLUCASBOOKS.COM
e-mail:samlucasbooks@btinternet.com

PUBLISHER - OSCAR PISCINE BOOKS

ACT 5, SCENE 1

8.31am. Saturday 18th October, 2025.
The streets of Moscow are bustling
with people jostling to get to work.
Outside the Bank of Russia, a taxi
pulls up and Felix Botkin steps out.
He is carrying his tatty briefcase and
has a Mackintosh raincoat over his
right forearm. He pays the taxi
driver, then walks inside the bank.
He shuffles down some steps clutching
his case and approaches a desk where a
woman is standing. He is very
nervous.

                    DESK WOMAN
Good morning, sir. Are you looking
to open a deposit box today?

                    FELIX BOTKIN
Yes, box 5237. Sorry, no, I mean box
5789. I always get that number mixed
up with an old bicycle padlock I had
when I was eight.

        (Felix Botkin is sweating and
        acting very nervous.)

                    DESK WOMAN
If you would just like to sign this
form...

*(The woman hands him a form
to sign, he signs it.)*

...Will you require a private booth
today, sir?

                    FELIX BOTKIN
No, I won't be very long.

          *(The woman hands him a piece
          of paper.)*

                    DESK WOMAN
If you just hand this piece of paper
to the guard at the door, he will let
you in so you can go to your box.

                    FELIX BOTKIN
Thank you.

          *(Felix Botkin hands the guard
          the piece of paper and is
          granted access to the safety
          deposit boxes. The guard
          locks the door behind him and
          Felix walks over to his box.
          He nervously opens his own
          safety deposit box and then
          quickly moves around the room
          to find Prime Minister
          Kantcoughsky's. He finds it,
          then frantically stabs at the
          lock with the key, opens it,
          grabs a gold disc and stuffs*

*it down his pants. He locks
up the safety deposit boxes
and walks over to the guard.
The guard opens the door and
Felix walks out. He walks
back up the stairs awkwardly
holding his briefcase and
pinching his knees together.
He makes it to the top and
then goes outside.)*

AGENT ORLOV
Felix Botkin?

*(Agent Orlov and Stepanov are
waiting outside the bank with
a car. The back door is
open. Felix Botkin stops
walking and drops his case.
He looks at agent Orlov.)*

FELIX BOTKIN
Yes?

AGENT ORLOV
You are under arrest.

FELIX BOTKIN
What for? You can't do this, I know
my rights, I'm a lawyer. What's the
charge?

*(Agent Stepanov walks behind
Felix, places him in*

*handcuffs and pushes him into
the back of the car along
with his briefcase and
raincoat. Stepanov gets in
the passenger seat and Orlov
the driver's. The car pulls
away.)*

                    AGENT ORLOV
What's the charge? Where do we
start? How about *accessory after the
fact* or *tampering with evidence*. And
I'm pretty sure once we get a look at
what you just removed from
Kantcoughsky's safety deposit box,
there will be a few more charges to
add to the list.

                    FELIX BOTKIN
Listen, Kantcoughsky made me do it.
I wanted nothing to do with his mess,
but...

          *(Felix pauses. He looks
          around at the buildings and
          people moving by.)*

                    AGENT ORLOV
But?

                    FELIX BOTKIN
Kantcoughsky has information
regarding a situation my son was
involved with a few years ago.

                    AGENT ORLOV
That would be the one with the
prostitute and the missing plastic
duck?

                    FELIX BOTKIN
How did you know about that?

                    AGENT ORLOV
We have Kantcoughsky's cell bugged.

                    FELIX BOTKIN
You can't do that, that's not right.
We were protected by the lawyer-
client privilege.

                    AGENT ORLOV
Maybe, but, the privilege is revoked
as soon as the lawyer, in this case
that is you, is involved with
committing or covering up a crime.
When you went to the bank to take the
storage disc from Kantcoughsky's
safety deposit box, you did both. If
I was you Felix, I would distance
yourself from Kantcoughsky and
cooperate with us a 100%. Who knows,
you might even get out a few hours to
see your son's wedding. Things could
be good for you Felix. All you have
to do is sign a piece of paper and
help us build a case against
Kantcoughsky. If you are lucky, you
might get off with 15 years hard

labour.

                    FELIX BOTKIN
15 years hard labour, get off with?

                    AGENT ORLOV
If you are lucky.

          (The car pulls up outside of
          the Penachy Jailhouse and
          Felix is escorted inside.
          Felix is shown into an
          interrogation room and his
          handcuffs are removed.)

                    AGENT STEPANOV
Hand over the disc Felix?

          (Felix removes the storage
          disc from his underpants and
          hands it to agent Stepanov.
          Agent Orlov takes out a large
          form and a pen and hands it
          to Felix.)

                    AGENT ORLOV
Sign this?

                    FELIX BOTKIN
What is it?

                    AGENT ORLOV
For you, it's a get out of jail free

card. Sign it and you can go.

                    FELIX BOTKIN
What do you mean, go?

                    AGENT ORLOV
Look, Felix, we are not interested in
you, we are interested in
Kantcoughsky and the man behind
Kantcoughsky...

          (Agent Orlov holds up the
          disc and looks at it. It is
          oddly different to most
          storage devices and is quite
          heavy and non-reflective.)

...If this disc has the information
on it we think it has, you have done
a great thing for the motherland.
Just sign the form and go to your
son's wedding. If you don't, we will
say you were shot trying to escape
and then agent Stepanov will plant a
gun on you and a large bag of
cocaine. What's it to be?

          (Felix becomes flustered and
          signs the form.)

                    FELIX BOTKIN
So, I can go?

                    AGENT ORLOV
Yes, of course...

          *(Felix gathers up his stuff
          and starts to leave.)*

...Oh, and Felix?

                    FELIX BOTKIN
Yes?

                    AGENT ORLOV
Don't say anything about this to
anyone and don't contact Kantcoughsky
again.

                    FELIX BOTKIN
Don't worry, I won't.

          (Felix leaves.)

                    AGENT STEPANOV
I'm hungry, you hungry?

                    AGENT ORLOV
Yeh, sure, I could eat.

Scene fades.

ACT 5, SCENE 2

8.45am, Saturday 18th October, 2025. Okan prison installation, level C. Outside the interrogation room, screaming and complaining continue to disturb the peace. Dmitry is still trying to pick Yuri's lock, but the lock is worn and old. They listen to the voices outside in the corridor.

GENERAL GERASIMOV
This is just stupid, you have been stuck to this moon person for 10 minutes.

GUARD 1
I am sorry General, but my shirt button is caught in his dress. Every time I move my arm a sequin or diamante falls off and he starts to scream.

GENERAL GERASIMOV
Just give it a good yank.

GUARD 1
I tried that, but the screaming is quite deafening, he really does have a high pitched squeal. I think I will have to see the doctor after this, I fear my malleus is stuck pounding my incus.

(*The General grabs the Moon Man and pulls him from the guard and throws him into the interrogation room. The Moon Man starts to sob.*)

MOON MAN

Swine. Just look at my dress, my aunt Agatha spent days sewing on those sequins, and you treat it like an old rag. You overstuffed chicken breast, think you're a right hard man don't you?

GENERAL GERASIMOV

Silence or I will cut out your tongue...

(*The General straightens his clothing and lights a cigar.*)

...Now, Yuri, where was I?

YURI

I believe, Vadim was crying at his father's grave.

GENERAL GERASIMOV

Yes, that is it. So, Vadim went to the back of the house to confront Mrs Rodriquez. She was sitting by the pool, drinking and laughing with a man. Vadim went up to her and showed her his mother's and father's rings,

which were now on his finger. He
pulled out a gun and asked them some
questions. After a lengthy
conversation, he discovered that Mrs.
Rodriguez had murdered her husband
while on holiday in Russia, but had
lost the body in the river after
strangulating him with a piano wire.
Without a body, she would not be able
to claim on his life insurance, so
when a body appeared at the morgue
the next day with her husband's
wallet, she stepped in and claimed
Yuri Schekov's body as his. After
Vadim heard her story, he shot her
along with the man and burnt the
house down.

                    YURI
What a terrible woman, I don't feel
so bad anymore.

                   DMITRY
That is good Yuri, and look on the
bright side, you had nothing to do
with the mother's death. The other
woman, that Mrs. Rodriguez, well, she
deserved to die.

                    YURI
Yes, she sounded like a real dirt
bag. You are right Dmitry, I can't
be held responsible for Vadim's
mother, she was dead before I even

met the other Yuri.

> *(The General can't believe
> his ears and starts to cough
> with the smoke from his
> cigar. Dmitry looks at the
> General. Yuri starts to pull
> at his handcuffs and they
> start to loosen.)*

                    DMITRY
General, there is one thing I don't
understand?

                    GENERAL GERASIMOV
What is that?

                    DMITRY
How Vadim found out about this
Yuri?...

> *(Dmitry points at Yuri.)*

...Yuri doesn't figure in your story?

                    GENERAL GERASIMOV
Vadim didn't find out about this
Yuri...

> *(The General points at Yuri.)*

...Until he came to work for me.
When he told me the story of his
childhood, I did a little

investigating and found out that a
Yuri Chekov joined the space academy
programme the same day Vadim's father
died. After cross referencing
addresses and some anomalous
information provided by this Yuri, I
discovered a bit more to the puzzle
and I knew something was wrong. The
further I looked, the more I
discovered. It would appear we now
have a full picture.

                    DMITRY
And I am glad it is sorted out.
There is nothing like clearing the
air.

                GENERAL GERASIMOV
Quite. Now, how did you return to
Earth?

        (The General grabs the Moon
        Man and puts the knife to his
        throat. Yuri's hands are now
        free but remain on the table.
        Dmitry looks on intently and
        is getting ready to move for
        the laser gun.)

                    YURI
Put him down and I will tell you...

        (The General lets the Moon
        Man go.)

...We hitched a ride on a cloud. Now
Dmitry.

> (Dmitry jumps from his seat
> and rushes the General. They
> fall to the floor and a
> struggle for the knife
> begins.)

                    GENERAL GERASIMOV
Take it! Please, don't hit me!

> (The General faints with
> fright and the knife falls on
> the floor.)

                    DMITRY
Quick, grab his knife.

> (Yuri picks up the knife and
> looks at the Moon Man.)

                    YURI
Are you alright?

                    MOON MAN
Yes thanks. Now what are we going
do?

                    YURI
Escape.

                    MOON MAN
Escape? How are we going do that, we
need fatty over there to work the
lift.

                    DMITRY
Did you hear everything Viktor was
telling me?

                    MOON MAN
Not everything, but enough to know we
need the General's hand to activate
the lift.

                    YURI
We will have to cut it off.

                    MOON MAN
Don't be so vulgar, he's not a lamb
chop. Let's take him with us, better
to have a hostage for a while,
somebody we can poke with a knife. I
don't know about you, but I like a
good prod.

                    YURI
Okay, we will call for the guard, and
when he comes in, you can do the
thing with your foot.

                    MOON MAN
What thing with my foot?

                    YURI
Y'know, the tripping up thing.

                  MOON MAN
Well, I've explained all that before.
It's not my fault you can't walk.

                    YURI
Are you going to do it or not?

                  MOON MAN
Well alright, don't get your knickers
in a twist.

                    YURI
Dmitry, let's pull the General's body
over there away from the door.

        *(Dmitry and Yuri move the
        General's body away from the
        entrance and the Moon Man
        waits behind the door.)*

                  DMITRY
Wait a minute!

        *(Dmitry goes over to the box
        and rummages around and pulls
        out a small bottle of whisky,
        takes a drink and puts the
        bottle in his pocket. He
        finds a packet of cigarettes
        and throws them over to Yuri.
        As the box moves, a single*

*Kopeck falls out and rolls
across the floor. Yuri picks
it up and puts it in his
pocket. Dmitry hides from
view.)*

YURI

A Kopeck is always good luck when it
comes to you.

DMITRY

Ready?

YURI

Ready.

DMITRY

Guard, come in here!

*(The door opens and the guard
trips over the Moon Man's
foot. Dmitry hits him over
the back of the head with a
chair and he stops moving.)*

MOON MAN

I think you've killed him?

DMITRY

I don't think so, but he will sleep
for a while...

> (*In the corner, the General
> starts to move.*)

...Get the General.

> (*Yuri moves over to the
> General and begins to pull
> him up.*)

YURI
He is a heavy lump, give me a hand.

> (*Dmitry helps get the General
> to his feet.*)

DMITRY
What a weight. I'll be glad when his
legs start moving by themselves.

Scene fades.

ACT 5, SCENE 3

8.53am. Saturday 18th October, 2025.
London and his team of ex-SAS soldiers
have spent a restless night on top of
a hill. London, Pilkington, Winslow
and Cartwright are fast asleep in a
small wooded area, Cavendish and
Carter are just returning from a
reconnoitre.

CAVENDISH
I don't believe this, just look at
them. The lazy sloths.

CARTER
Just as well we're not the Russian
army. They'd all be dead by now.

LONDON
Maybe not.

*(London appears from behind
Carter and holds a twig to
his throat.)*

CARTER
'Ere, hold up. Watch what you're
doing with that twig.

CAVENDISH
So, you weren't asleep then?

                    LONDON
On the contrary Cavendish, drawing
the enemy into close quarters is the
best plan of action when you don't
have suitable weaponry.

          *(Cavendish looks at the rest
          of the men sleeping.)*

                  CAVENDISH
What about this lot?

                   LONDON
Yes, well, I'm afraid they went back
to sleep. You chaps have been gone a
jolly long time. Did you find
anything of interest.

                  CAVENDISH
Yes, we're on an island.

                   LONDON
An island? That's impossible, we're
hundreds of miles from the coast.

                  CAVENDISH
Maybe so, but this little hill of
yours is separated by 50 yards of
water in every direction.

                   LONDON
50 yards you say. Doesn't sound a
lot?

CAVENDISH
No it doesn't, and if we were
walking, you could probably do it in
2 minutes, but this is water. Water
that's in Russia in October.

LONDON
Right, I get your point Cavendish.
Mmm, well yes, it's a conundrum
that's for sure. I guess we better
wake the others up and see what they
think.

        *(London walks over to the
        others.)*

LONDON
Pilky, Winslow, Cartwright? On your
feet?...

        *(Slowly they move and stand
        around London.)*

...Right, listen up chaps. I'm
afraid Cavendish and Carter have
discovered some troublesome news.

WINSLOW
What is it now, did you forget to
order the pickled onion with me fish
and chips? They always forget the
pickled onion.

                    LONDON
Very funny Winslow, but seriously we
have a slight problem. We're on an
island.

                    WINSLOW
We're what?

                    LONDON
On an island.

                    CARTWRIGHT
But we must be hundreds of miles from
the coast, how can that be?

                    LONDON
Look chaps, I'm only going by what
Cavendish has told me.

                    CAVENDISH
You calling me a liar?

                    LONDON
No, that's not what I am saying.

                    CAVENDISH
Then what are you saying?

          (London reaches inside his
          tunic and pulls out his map.)

                    LONDON
Nothing. Let's look at the map. Now

you have discovered we're surrounded
by water, it should be easy to
find...

        (*London moves his finger over
        the map.*)

...Look! Here we are, and this is
the lake. Lake Melkoye Vody.

                    PILKINGTON
So, how deep is the lake?

                    LONDON
Don't know Pilky, but as Cavendish
pointed out earlier, it's October and
the water is a trifle cold.

                    WINSLOW
Could we not build a raft?

                    LONDON
A raft? Does anyone know anything
about raft building?

                    PILKY
I built a boat out of *lolly* sticks
once.

                    LONDON
Did you Pilky, how did you get on?

PILKY
It sank, I failed to take into
account the tidal condition of the
area and it smashed against the
rocks.

LONDON
Well at least we don't have that
problem here. I suggest we make our
way down to the water's edge and
investigate for ourselves.

WINSLOW
Do you think there will be any chance
of breakfast this morning?

LONDON
That rather depends if we can get
across that lake.

WINSLOW
I hope so, I'm feeling quite faint.

LONDON
Best not to think about it Winslow.

WINSLOW
Alright, I'll try. What shall I
think about instead.

LONDON
That's up to you...

> (*London points at the
> ground.*)

...Whilst your thinking about
something to think about, you can
pick up that metal bar and those
green crystals. You never know when
they might come in handy.

                    WINSLOW
Alright.

> (*They all walk down to the
> water's edge and look across
> to the next shore.*)

                    CARTWRIGHT
Look there, a boat!

> (*On the other side of the
> lake is a rowing boat moored
> up.*)

                    LONDON
You're right Cartwright. All we need
now is someone to bring it to us.

                    CAVENDISH
Shall we call for a policeman?

                    LONDON
Alright Cavendish, there's no need
for that. One of us will have to go
and get it that's all.

                    CAVENDISH
Any volunteers?

                    LONDON
I suppose, I will have to get it.
I'm a pretty good swimmer, got the
old bronze medallion back at school.
It's not that far, I'll just strip
down to the old underwear, swim over
and row back and get you chaps.

                    CAVENDISH
That water's freezing, you'll die of
hyperthermia.

                    LONDON
Well maybe Pilky could light a fire
and when I get back I'll warm up in
no time.

                    CAVENDISH
Light a fire? Have you forgotten
what happened the last time?

                    LONDON
Oh, yes, did cause rather a stir.
Can't say I want those fellows on our
back again, what? Look, I'll just
have to be quick that's all. As long
as I have warm clothes to put on when
I get back and dry myself off
properly I should be fine...

          (*London starts to undress and*

*goes down to his underwear.
He walks into the water and
runs back out yelping. His
teeth start to chatter.)*

...It's, it's freezing! Ca...can't
be...lieve how co...cold it is.

                    CAVENDISH
I told you, it's suicide.

                     LONDON
Well, I'm no...not go...going to
gi... give up.

          *(London runs towards the lake
          and dives in only to face-
          plant and still be on the
          surface. He gets back up and
          walks back to the shore
          rubbing his face.)*

                    CAVENDISH
Not very deep is it, I bet I could
walk across.

          *(Cavendish takes off his
          shoes and socks and rolls up
          his trousers. He starts to
          walk to the other side.
          Before too long he is over
          halfway there.)*

WINSLOW
It looks like he's going to make it.

LONDON
Yes, it does...

     (Cavendish makes it to the
     other side.)

...Looks like we won't be needing
that boat after all. Take off your
shoes and socks, and I'll see you on
the other side.

     (London and the rest of the
     ex-SAS walk over to the other
     side of the water, sit down
     on the bank and get dressed.)

PILKINGTON
What's the plan now?

LONDON
Plan? Oh, yes. Well, I suggest we
take a quick look at the old map and
make our way to the nearest town or
village...

     (London pulls out the map.)

...Gather round chaps...

     (London runs his finger along
     the map.)

...We are here, so I suggest we make
our way to this place called *Dry
Oakov*. Looks pretty small, nothing
more than a village I would say, but
it's the closest thing on the map to
our location. It looks to be about
10 miles away, so it's a bit of a
hike on an empty stomach. Probably
won't even be much there, a few sheep
farmers and the odd social worker.
If we are lucky, we might find a car
or a phone.

                    WINSLOW
So, no breakfast then?

                    LONDON
No Winslow, I'm afraid not, but if we
cover the ground quickly, we should
be in time for lunch. Looks like
there is no water in the way, so it's
more or less a straight line. Right
let's get going.

            *(London and his team of ex-
            SAS soldiers walk over the
            first hill and are confronted
            with a huge piece of the
            alien vessel. It appears to
            be part of the bridge and the
            hyper drive system. Two big
            gold doors stick out of the
            landscape along with gears*

*and cogs. They poke out
above the rocks and trees
glistening in the morning
sun.)*

                    CARTWRIGHT
Look at the size of that, it's
amazing!

                    LONDON
I think we've hit the mother lode
chaps.

                    CAVENDISH
I don't think we can carry that home
with us.

        *(They start to walk amongst
        the broken vessel.)*

                    PILKINGTON
It reminds me of my father's old
grandfather clock. He was always
taking it apart and putting it back
together. He'd know what all this
stuff was.

                    CARTER
Still looks like a load of old
rubbish to me, I mean brass cogs to
cross the boundaries of space. What
did they do, wind it up with a big
key?

LONDON
Carter. You failed to recognise anything good in the Russian tent of alien artefacts whilst Winslow saved the day. I suggest you address your attitude and try and be of some use. There must be something of importance in amongst the wreckage. Go over to those big gold doors and investigate that area.

CARTER
Alright, but I'm not fillin' my bleedin' pockets with cogs and gears.

> *(They all search amongst the vessel for a few minutes and grab various pieces of gears, knobs and poles.)*

CARTER
Oi, come an' 'ave a butchers at this!

> *(The group of men walk over to Carter.)*

LONDON
I hope this is of some use Carter...

> *(The men stand in front of the two gold doors that used to go to the ship's bridge. They are broken and melted, but in the centre of the*

door, in pristine condition,
lies the gold Medallion of
Life.)

...Well Carter, I must say, you get
full marks for this. What a
spectacular artefact. Looks like
precious stones: diamonds, emeralds,
sapphires and amethysts all encased
in a medallion of gold...

(London looks at the
medallion closer and puts his
hands on it.)

...I think if I give it a twist it
might come out...

(London gives the medallion a
twist and it falls into his
hand.)

...There...

(London holds it up into the
morning sunshine.)

...Truly magnificent.

                    CARTER
Yeh, it is nice. Now, can I have it
back.

                    LONDON
Have it back?

(London looks at Carter.)

CARTER
Yes, I found it, it's mine. Finders
keepers.

LONDON
This isn't yours Carter, this is
going back to MI5 so they can study
it. They're funding this expedition.

CARTER
Funding? Don't make me laugh. We
came here with the barest of
equipment and provisions. We never
had any food or drink and we haven't
even got a bleedin' ride home. I bet
you we end up at Moscow train station
paying for a trip back to Croydon.

LONDON
I don't think things are as quite as
bad as that Carter. When we get to
town, I will radio HQ and organise a
new pick up point. Now, you can hold
on to that medallion for the time
being, but when we get home you are
going to have to turn it over.

CARTER
We'll see.

LONDON
Carter, not everything in life is
fair. Perhaps I can get you a
finder's fee, five pounds or
something.

CARTER

Five pounds?

LONDON
Alright ten, but not a penny more.

WINSLOW

What about me?

LONDON
What do you mean Winslow?

WINSLOW
Will I get something for the green
crystals?

LONDON
Yes, I'm sure I can come up with
something, a bag of *Barley Twists* or
Army & Navy.

WINSLOW
Barley Twists?

LONDON
Yes, a true taste of happiness...

(*London hands over the
medallion to Carter.*)

...Right, now that's all settled, I
suggest we get going. That Russian
patrol could still be looking for us
and now that we have something of
value, I'd rather the enemy didn't
get their hands on it...

(*They move off into the
woods. London turns to
Carter*)

...And remember Carter?

(*Carter examines the
medallion with interest.*)

                    CARTER
What?

                    LONDON
I want that back when we get home.

                    CARTER
We'll see.

Scene fades.

ACT 5, SCENE 4

In the timeless depths of space, the EgÁsian reconnaissance ship, *The Red Neval,* hurtles towards Earth at an astonishing rate. On board, are the autopilot KAL and an uninvited guest. A dark figure staggers onto the bridge holding his head. KAL is at an instrument panel plotting the fastest route to Earth.

                    MACTAVISH
Ye alright there pal? Pure dead brilliant ship this, travels through the air and nae the sea.

          *(KAL is startled and turns to
          face MacTavish. KAL is a
          much earlier version of SAL
          and is a kinetic energy based
          life form. He is dressed in
          white and is an albino.
          MacTavish is drunk and can
          barely stand.)*

                      KAL
Who are you? What are you doing on this ship?

                    MACTAVISH
It was a mishanter, I was keekin for a cludgie.

                    KAL
Sorry, but I am having difficulty
understanding your dialect. I will
just access the EgÁsian data bank on
languages. Accessing... Data
flow... Uplink complete. I see, you
are from the highland region.

                  MACTAVISH
Aye.

                    KAL
And you were looking for the
bathroom?

                  MACTAVISH
Aye, that's right.

      (MacTavish stumbles towards
      KAL.)

                    KAL
Where have you been up until now,
we've been travelling nearly a day?

                  MACTAVISH
Och, I knocked mysel' oot when this
thing took aff into the air. I
banged ma head on a cupboard.

                    KAL
Well, you don't appear to have
sustained major damage.

                    MACTAVISH
Na, just a wee scrape.   Ma head's as
tough as a plank.

                       KAL
Good.

                    MACTAVISH
See, if we've been goin' nearly a
day, we must be near the muckle toon?

       (MacTavish moves closer to
       KAL.)

                       KAL
Near the City?

                    MACTAVISH
Aye.

                       KAL
I'm afraid we are nowhere near a
city, we are entering a new galaxy
called the Milky Way, well at least
that's what the Earthlings call it.

                    MACTAVISH
Earthlings?

                       KAL
Yes, they live on a funny flat planet
millions of miles away from EgÁs, but
that's where the Medallion of Life is

and that's my mission.

                    MACTAVISH
So, we are nae on EgÁs anymore?

                    KAL
No. We left there some hours ago. I
think you misunderstand the purpose
of this ship. It doesn't traverse
air, we're in space. This is a
spaceship.

                    MACTAVISH
Spaceship?

                    KAL
Yes, take a look.

          (MacTavish walks over to the
          window and sees the universe
          flying by at great speed.)

It's full o' stars?

                    KAL
Yes, billions of them.

                    MACTAVISH
And you're heading tae Earth tae get
the Medallion of Lee?

                    KAL
That's right. A few more hours and

we will be there.

MACTAVISH
And then we'll be goin' back hame?

KAL
Yes, that's right.

MACTAVISH
A'richt then. A few hours on a
strange planet tae keek at the talent
and then back hame. I can handle
that.

(MacTavish does a strange
dance then looks at KAL.)

KAL
Good. I trust I can call on your
assistance if I require help in
obtaining the Medallion of Life?

MACTAVISH
Nae problem, I'm your jimmy.

KAL
Very good. I'm afraid I can't offer
you any food or drink, this ship has
been in storage for over five
thousand years.

MACTAVISH
Don't worry yoursel' about me pal,

I've brought ma own...

> *(MacTavish pulls out a fine*
> *alcoholic beverage called*
> *'Wherth' from the highlands*
> *of EgÁs and takes a drink.*
> *He looks closer at KAL.)*

... If you don't mind me saying, ye
seem a bitty aff colour? Are you a
bit under the weather?

                    KAL
No, I'm fine. Cotton white is my
normal colour. I'm not real, I'm a
kinetic based life form.

                    MACTAVISH
Kinetic?

                    KAL
The motion of the ship gives me life.

                    MACTAVISH
Aye, really interesting, will ye have
a dram?

                    KAL
I'm afraid, I'm unable to.

                    MACTAVISH
That's a pity, bit aye more for me.
I usually don't trust an EgÁsian that

doesn't drink, bit ye seem alright.

                    KAL
Well, thank you.

                 MACTAVISH
If it's all the same to ye, I'm off
tae have a wee kip. Wake me up when
we get there.

        (MacTavish finds a seat,
        slumps into it and starts to
        drink.)

                    KAL
Yes, will do.

Scene fades.

ACT 5, SCENE 5

9.04am. Saturday 18th October, 2025.
Okan prison installation. Outside in
the corridor, Dmitry, Yuri and the
Moon Man quickly shuffle along pulling
General Gerasimov between them. On
the speakers, a song can be heard -
'The Girl from Ipanema'.

                GENERAL GERASIMOV
You'll never get away with this.
This installation is escape proof.

        *(Up ahead, a motorised cart
        lies empty.)*

                    DMITRY
Shut up and get in...

        *(Dmitry pushes the General
        into the back seat of the
        cart. Yuri gets in the back
        with him and holds the laser
        gun on him. The Moon Man
        joins Dmitry in the front.
        Dmitry drives off.)*

...Hold on to your seats!

        *(Ahead, two armed guards come
        into view. Dmitry speeds
        up.)*

                    GENERAL GERASIMOV
I told you, you are done for.

                         YURI
Keep quiet, we can always leave you
here and take your hand with us!

          *(The two guards realise an
          escape is in progress and
          shout out.)*

                        GUARD
Stop or I'll shoot!

          (Dmitry speeds up.)

                       DMITRY
Hold on, I can see the lift. I am
going to ram these two...

          *(The guards begin to shoot,
          but then jump out of the way.
          Dmitry flies past them and
          crashes into the wall by the
          lift.)*

...Is everyone okay?

                         YURI
My teeth are a little looser, but I
will survive.

                       MOON MAN
I've broken my heal, this day keeps

getting worse.

                    DMITRY
Quickly, get the General in the lift.

          *(They all move into the lift
          and the door closes. The
          guards get back on their feet
          and start shooting at the
          lift. The bullets do not
          penetrate, but an indentation
          is made. An alarm sounds
          out.)*

              GENERAL GERASIMOV
That's it, it is all over. No one
can leave now.

                    DMITRY
Shut up.

          *(A voice is heard in the
          lift.)*

                    VOICE
Security protocol Foxtrot-Echo has
been activated. Total Lock-down of
the Okan prison will initiate in two
minutes.

          *(Dmitry addresses the
          General.)*

                    DMITRY
Put your hand on the screen.

              GENERAL GERASIMOV
You are wasting your time.

                    DMITRY
Shut up and put your hand on the
screen or I will have Yuri cut it
off.

          *(The General places his hand
          on the screen.)*

                    VOICE
Welcome General Gerasimov. What
level please?

                    DMITRY
Level A

                    VOICE
Sorry, voice not recognised. Please
state your Level?

          *(Yuri pushes the laser gun
          into the General's back.)*

              GENERAL GERASIMOV
Level A

          (The lift begins to rise.)

                    MOON MAN
I'm glad we didn't just take his
hand.

                     YURI
Yes, so am I.

               GENERAL GERASIMOV
Give up now, and I will kill you
quickly. You can't get out of the
building, you need to know the
password to open the main door.

                    DMITRY
That is alright, you can tell us.

               GENERAL GERASIMOV
I can't.

                    DMITRY
Then I will make you.

               GENERAL GERASIMOV
I mean, I can't. I don't know it.
As a security measure, senior staff
members and high ranking officers are
not told the current password. When
someone wants to break out, they
always grab the most senior member of
staff. So, as a precaution, we are
not told. At the moment, I believe
there are only four members of
security here that know the password

and as soon as the alarm is sounded
they are instantly moved to level F
under armed guard. There are usually
six, but your little escape from our
convoy two nights ago left two of
them dead. Sgt, Smithsky was one of
our best officers. I can tell you,
General Spuriovsky was most upset
over your escape and the death of so
many fine officers, it ruined his
night of bridge.

> *(The lift comes to a stop and
> the doors begin to open.)*

                    YURI
Did you say Sergeant Smithsky?

> *(Yuri looks out of the lift.
> The coast is clear.)*

                    GENERAL GERASIMOV
Yes.

> *(They all walk out of the
> lift and down a corridor
> towards a big metal door.
> Two armed guards wait in an
> office area just in front of
> the door.)*

                    DMITRY
Funny, I expected more guards?

                    GENERAL GERASIMOV
I told you, no one can escape the
main entrance. No one on this level
knows the password, they are all on
level F. You are stuck, even if you
get past the two guards you cannot go
anywhere.

                    DMITRY
That stupid Popov, he said you would
know the password.

                    GENERAL GERASIMOV
Well, I don't.

                    MOON MAN
So, this is it, is it?

          (Yuri is muttering some words
          to himself over and over.)

                    DMITRY
Yuri, what are you doing?

                    YURI
I am trying to remember what the
Sergeant said.

                    DMITRY
What Sergeant?

                    YURI
Sergeant Smithsky. He told us

something before he died. It seemed
like nonsense at the time, but maybe
he was helping us. Maybe he realised
who we were.

                    DMITRY
He was dying Yuri. Forget about
that. Give me the gun...

        *(Yuri hands Dmitry the laser
        gun. Dmitry grabs The
        General and starts to walk
        towards the guards.)*

...I have the General, come out of
the office with your arms up or I
will shoot?

        *(The two guards look out of
        the office and see the
        General. They walk out with
        their hands up.)*

               VOICE OVER TANNOY
30 seconds to complete lock down.

                    DMITRY
You two on the floor.

                GENERAL GERASIMOV
It's over, give up! It is pointless
to keep going, you are embarrassing
yourselves.

(*Yuri scribbles down some words on a piece of paper and hands it to the General.*)

YURI

Here, walk over to the door and say this.

GENERAL GERASIMOV

What, I won't do it.

DMITRY

What's going on Yuri.

YURI

I think I have the password, but we need him to say it.

VOICE

10 seconds before lock down.

(*Dmitry shoots the General in the left foot, he cries out. Dmitry grabs the General, takes him over to the door and stamps on his left foot.*)

DMITRY

Read the lines.

GENERAL GERASIMOV

Honest Frank is forthcoming and candid.

VOICE OVER TANNOY
Thank you General Gerasimov. Opening
main door. Lock down in 5 seconds...

*(The door opens to create a
small gap then stops.)*

...Initiating lock down. Door
closing.

DMITRY
Yuri, quick.

*(Dmitry pushes the General
out of the way. Yuri grabs
the Moon Man and they all
squeeze through the door.
Seconds later, the door
closes. Outside, the
brightness of a new morning
greets them.)*

MOON MAN
We did it, we did it...

(The Moon Man looks at Yuri.)

...Oh, you are ever so clever,
imagine you remembering an unknown
password. I could never remember
something I didn't know, I have
trouble remembering things I do know.

YURI
Yes, it was a good trick. What now
Dmitry?

DMITRY
We have got to get out of here...

> *(Outside, Yuri, Dmitry and
> the Moon Man find themselves
> amongst old tenement
> buildings and a disused
> industrial estate. The road
> is broken up and weeds grow
> everywhere. The whole place
> looks abandoned. A hundred
> yards down the road, a light
> blue 1971 Volkswagen
> caravanette is parked up.
> Under the back wheel is a
> house brick.)*

...Let's try that camper.

> *(As they walk closer to the
> camper, they can see it is in
> a bad state of repair.)*

YURI
I don't fancy our chances with this
one Dmitry. Even the handbrake is a
house brick.

DMITRY
Let's try it anyway...

> *(Dmitry tries the doors but
> they are locked.)*

...The keys are in the ignition but
the doors are locked.

                    YURI
I have an idea...

> *(Yuri takes out his lucky
> Kopeck and puts it in the
> lock and wiggles it.)*

...I remember my father doing this to
his old car when I was boy. He was
always locking his keys inside.
Locks were pretty bad back then.

> *(Yuri twist the Kopeck and
> the door opens.)*

...There!

                    DMITRY
It really is a lucky Kopeck...

> *(Dmitry jumps in the camper
> and tries to start it but the
> battery is flat and the
> engine just moans in pain.)*

...Give me a push, it might start if
you push me.

                    MOON MAN
Oh, I don't push campers, it will
ruin my nails...

         (Behind them, shots ring out
         and the main door begins to
         open.)

...On second thoughts.

         (Yuri and the Moon Man start
         to push the camper.)

                    DMITRY
That is good, but push faster...

         (Yuri and the Moon Man push
         harder.)

...I am going to let out the clutch.

         (The camper coughs and
         splutters, kangaroos for a
         moment and then starts.
         Dmitry pulls forward then
         stops.)

...Get in.

         (Yuri and the Moon Man jump
         in. Yuri is carrying the
         house brick and shows it to
         Dmitry.)

                    YURI
We better take this just in case you
have to do a hill start.

          *(Shots spray past them as
          they disappear down the
          road.)*

                    DMITRY
Yes, a hill start can be tricky
without a house brick.

                    YURI
Do you know where we are Dmitry?

                    DMITRY
Not exactly, but I believe we are
about two or three hours away from
Moscow on the south side...

          *(Up ahead there is a security
          station with a boom barrier.
          A patrol jeep is parked
          outside next to a guard box.)*

...Hold on, I am not stopping.

          *(They crash through the
          barrier and a guard emerges
          from a small cubical holding
          a newspaper and a pickled
          cabbage sandwich. He drops
          them and jumps into the jeep
          and starts to follow the*

campervan at great speed.)

YURI
He is following us.

DMITRY
I don't think we will be able to out run him. Throw anything you can find out the back window to slow him down.

(Yuri breaks the back window with the house brick and starts to throw stuff out: seats, cushions, rugs, blankets, books, water bottles, tins of food, the house brick and an aquarium. The jeep steers to avoid the debris and speeds up bashing into their bumper. The guard takes out his gun and starts to shoot.)

YURI
Sorry Dmitry, I have lost the handbrake.

DMITRY
Don't worry, I do not want to stop just now.

(The Moon Man throws a stuffed toy at the jeep and stares at the driver.)

                    MOON MAN
Oh, what a horrible little man, why
doesn't he just go away. I don't
like men with thin moustaches, there
is something wrong with them.

                      YURI
The man's moustache is the least of
our worries.

                    MOON MAN
Even so, it's very distracting.

                     DMITRY
How's it going back there?

                      YURI
We are running out of stuff.

                     DMITRY
You better do something quickly, the
engine is getting very hot.

          *(Yuri pulls out the cutlery
          draw and throws it out of the
          back window. It breaks the
          glass to the jeep's
          windscreen and a knife goes
          into the driver's neck. The
          jeep careers off the road and
          into a ditch.)*

                    MOON MAN
You did it. Oh, you two are ever so
exciting. If I didn't smell so bad,
I'd be quite enjoying meself.

                     YURI
Dmitry, he is gone. You can slow
down.

                    DMITRY
Good, I think the engine is about to
blow. We better stop a minute...

     (Dmitry pulls over.)

...I would turn it off, but we
wouldn't get it started again.

                     YURI
We better think quick. Gerasimov
must have the word out on us by now.
We need a plan.

                    DMITRY
I am fed up with needing a plan, what
do you suggest?

                     YURI
We must contact the police and tell
them the Penachy County Jail is about
to be blown up by a terrorist...

     (Yuri looks around.)

...and we must try and get back to
Moscow.

> DMITRY
Why, what is in Moscow?

> YURI
The card to the camcorder.

> DMITRY
What card?

> YURI
The one General Gerasimov wants.

> DMITRY
Oh, that card. The one that was
missing from the camcorder?

> YURI
Yes.

> DMITRY
I have to confess, I am a little
confused concerning the exact
whereabouts of that card. I knew
your story about a flat battery was
bogus, but I have to admit, the whole
thing is a complete mystery to me.

> YURI
I changed over card on alien
spaceship, just after you'd taken

footage of Earth; it was full up.
When we handed it to Press, I had
forgotten I'd changed it.

                    DMITRY
So where is card now?

                    YURI
My little tartan bear has it inside
of his tummy.

                    DMITRY
Your bear?...

     (Dmitry starts to laugh.)

Your bear has it, and you gave it to
the girl scout...

     (Dmitry continues to laugh
      and Yuri joins him.)

...Yuri, that is the best mistake you
have done yet.

                    YURI
Better than Boris?

                    DMITRY
Yes, better than Boris. C'mon let 's
go.

                    MOON MAN
What's happening?

                    DMITRY
We are going to Moscow to find a
bear!

Scene fades.

ACT 6, SCENE 1

10.21am. Saturday 18th October, 2025.
Penachy Jailhouse, Moscow, Russia.
Inside the Jail, Agents Orlov and
Stepanov   are   questioning   Prime
Minister Kantcoughsky again.   He is
not happy and wants to see his lawyer.

P.M. KANTCOUGHSKY
Look, I don't understand why we are
here again. I told you I would not
speak to you without my lawyer
present. When Felix gets here, I
will answer your questions.

AGENT STEPANOV
I'm afraid Felix isn't coming.

P.M. KANTCOUGHSKY
What do you mean?

AGENT STEPANOV
Felix has decided not to represent
you anymore.

P.M. KANTCOUGHSKY
Why?

AGENT ORLOV
It would seem he has a very important
wedding to go to and he no longer
wishes to represent you.

                    AGENT STEPANOV
His son's I believe.

                    P.M. KANTCOUGHSKY
This must be your doing.

                    AGENT ORLOV
Not really, it was more you than us.

                    P.M. KANTCOUGHSKY
What does that mean?

                    AGENT ORLOV
It means that, after he was caught
with a certain storage disc which was
removed from a certain safety deposit
box early this morning, he was only
too willing to help the K.G.B with
its investigation against you and
your associates. In fact, he signed
an affidavit stating as much.

          *(Agent Orlov pulls out the
          affidavit and waves it in
          front of Kantcoughsky.)*

                    P.M. KANTCOUGHSKY
So, you have the disc from my safety
deposit box?

                    AGENT ORLOV
Yes, we have it. It is currently
with our encryption team at the

moment. I would imagine they will
get past your security protocols
within the next few hours and then we
will have enough information to make
you and your friends very comfortable
at Butrayka prison for a long time.

                    P.M. KANTCOUGHSKY
The disc will not give you any
information about my friends or
myself, it's not what you think.

                    AGENT ORLOV
So, it won't tell us the location of
a certain plastic duck?

          *(Kantcoughsky starts to
          laugh.)*

                    P.M. KANTCOUGHSKY
You were bugging my cell, what a
waste of time. That was complete
rubbish I told Felix so he would get
the disc. His son was cleared of
those allegations regarding the dead
prostitute. I don't have any harmful
information on anyone, I just tell
people stories so they will help me.
It's just a laugh. The people think
I have a hold over them and they
commit a criminal act on my behalf.
It works time and time again and my
hands remain clean.

                    AGENT STEPANOV
So, what is on the disc?

                  P.M. KANTCOUGHSKY
I suppose there is no harm in telling
you, you will find out soon enough...

        *(Kantcoughsky sits back in
        his chair.)*

...I know by your tie pins you have a
clearance level B5, so I can tell
you. The disc contains information
about the Chinese and the American
Space Program. As you know, five
years ago the Americans formed a
coalition with the Chinese. This
coalition's main objective was to
breach the Dome and make contact with
the alien vessel on the other side.
This was something that the Russian
government could not allow to happen.
If the Americans and the Chinese were
to gain access to alien technology,
there would be a shift in world
power. Before long, our great nation
would be second fiddle to their bow.
Six months ago, a plan was
implemented to speed up our own space
program. This meant we needed to
first thwart their efforts. Once we
had learnt they intended to use the
International Space Station as a
launching pad for their new vessel,
we had no alternative but to blow it

up. We just had to make it look like
an accident. It was a great solution
to a difficult problem.

                (Agent Orlov leans back and
                looks at Agent Stepanov and
                then back to Kantcoughsky.)

                AGENT ORLOV
What about the Four Seasons hotel,
Why was that blown up?

                P.M. KANTCOUGHSKY
I cannot tell you that, you know too
much already. After you have
decrypted the disc, I will be
released from this place without
charge.

                AGENT STEPANOV
What do you mean?

                P.M. KANTCOUGHSKY
Once your superiors learn the disc in
their possession is not the one they
think it is, they will release me.

                AGENT STEPANOV
I don't understand?

                P.M. KANTCOUGHSKY
I am sure you don't. The storage

disc you have does contain the information I have just told you, along with much, much more. You will find detailed data and schematics on advanced weaponry and aircraft that the Americans and Chinese have. You will also see blue prints for a new vessel they are developing to travel into space. 100's of documents and photos on secret programs like the weather laser at the CLARSACHS institute in Scotland, launch codes for nuclear weapons and walkthroughs for classic arcade games. It even has the eleven secret herbs and spices for KFC, but it doesn't have the information your superiors are looking for. They are looking for something quite different altogether.

(Agent Orlov leans forward.)

                    AGENT ORLOV
You wanted Felix to get caught with the disc?

                  P.M. KANTCOUGHSKY
Of course. He is an idiot, you can't trust him to do anything. He is also a coward, an easy target - very exploitable, my favourite kind of guy.

                    AGENT ORLOV
So, you think once our superiors look
at the disc you will be set free?

                  P.M. KANTCOUGHSKY
Yes. I have only been in jail this
long because they think they can
steal the information from me. When
they find out it is not on the disc,
they will set me free and pretend it
was a mistake.

                    AGENT ORLOV
You can't possibly hope to get out of
jail, everyone knows you were
involved in the bombing of the Four
Seasons hotel. Olga confessed on
camera that you ordered a Pizza from
your hotel room to be delivered the
following day at 7am. The exact time
you were rescued.

                  P.M. KANTCOUGHSKY
It might seem suspicious to most
people, but not unexplainable. Trust
me gentlemen, in a few hours I will
be free and you will be reassigned to
another case. My recommendation to
you is you take it without
question...

            *(Outside the interrogation
            room a big explosion occurs.
            Lights flicker and dust seeps*

under the door.)

...What's happening?

*(Alarms go off and then a
devastating explosion
destroys the entrance to the
building and the ground
floor. Debris and grey dust
cover everything and burst
water pipes create fountains
in the carnage and spew out
through a mountain of
concrete and metal. Outside
the Penachy County Jail,
people stare on in disbelief
and begin to cry and moan.
One of the spectators looks
on at the fallen jailhouse
and smiles. He walks away
from the scene and gets into
a car. He adjusts the rear
view mirror, starts the
engine and drives away. The
man is Vadim Schekov.)*

Scene Fades.

ACT 6, SCENE 2

11.07am. Saturday 18th October, 2025.
Five miles south from the village of
Dry Oakov, Smolank Oblast Russia.
London and his group of ex-SAS
soldiers have been walking for over 2
hours and they are quite tired. They
have been up hills and they have been
down hills, through woodlands and open
spaces. They now find themselves in
amongst tall pine trees heading
towards an open field. Cavendish is
at Point and is leading the way.
Winslow is complaining about his
stomach and Cartwright is starting to
drag his left leg.

                    WINSLOW
Do you think pine cones are edible?

        (*Winslow is playing with a
        pine cone in his hands as he
        walks.*)

                    LONDON
I think they are quite poisonous
Winslow. They probably won't kill
you, but they will make you sick and
leave you feeling quite depressed.

                    WINSLOW
I already feel really depressed,
quite depressed would be an

improvement.

                    LONDON
Come, come Winslow, things aren't all
that bad. We've managed to
accomplish our mission and we've
evaded capture from the Russians. I
would say things are on the up and
up.

          *(Ahead, in the open field in
          front of them, the sound of a
          radio can be heard.)*

                  CAVENDISH
Be quiet, I hear something.

          (A radio is playing music.)

                   CARTER
That sounds like music...

          (Carter listens intently)

...it is. Sounds like The 5th
Dimension. Great song, just got to
number one last week, saw it on *Top
of the Pops*.

                  CAVENDISH
Aye, that's great, but where's it
coming from.

          (London puts his left hand up

*and points to the field in
front of them.)*

LONDON
It's coming from that field, and I
hear voices.

CARTWRIGHT
Russians?

LONDON
No, I think it's Germans.

CAVENDISH
Germans?

LONDON
Yes, no mistaking those vowel sounds.

WINSLOW
What are the Germans doing here?

LONDON
Winslow, people do go on holiday to
other countries.

WINSLOW
Yes, I know, but Germans?

LONDON
Ssh!

*(London and his group of ex-
SAS soldiers move closer
towards the opening to get a
closer look. In front of
them sit a man and a woman on
a blanket. They are having a
picnic - Wine, cheese,
strawberries, smoked ham,
salami, potato salad, boiled
eggs, lettuce, tomatoes and a
loaf of pumpernickel lay out
on a serving board. The man
is dressed in Lederhosen and
the woman a Dirndl. Behind
the couple is a hot air
balloon anchored to the
ground by 3 ropes. The
balloon's design is made up
of 3 horizontal stripes:
black, red and yellow covered
by a rope net attached to a
wicker basket. For ballast,
small bags of sand hang from
the sides.)*

                CARTER
Perhaps we should steal that balloon?

                LONDON
You just can't take things because
they are there Carter, we're not at
war. These people have done nothing
to us. No, the best thing to do is
to stay quiet and move on. We can
only be a few miles from Dry Oakov.

                    CARTWRIGHT
Didn't sound like there would be much
there, just more walking after a
rest. A balloon ride does sound
nice, perhaps we could ask them for a
lift to the nearest town?

                     LONDON
Cartwright, it may have slipped your
mind, but we are in this country
illegally. If we get caught, we will
be shot as spies.

                    CARTWRIGHT
My left leg's playing up at the
moment, if we don't get on that
balloon, I fear the worst.

                     LONDON
Cartwright, you are such a drama
queen. You were in the SAS for
Pete's sake, what happened to
overcoming all obstacles to complete
your mission?

                    CARTWRIGHT
Age. I got old.

                     LONDON
Yes, well. None of us are as young
as we used to be, but a soldier's
duty is to perform to the best of his
or her ability at all times. Isn't
that right Pilky?...

(Pilkington doesn't answer
and seems to be missing from
the group.)

...I say, has anyone seen Pilky?

CARTER
Last I saw of him was five minutes
ago when we stopped to look at this
field and heard the Germans.

(At that moment, Pilkington
comes running up from the
rear.)

PILKINGTON
Ever so sorry lads, but I fell asleep
on that rock back there. Didn't
realise you'd moved on.

LONDON
Pilky, do try and keep up.
Everyone's tired. What would happen
if we all just fell asleep on a rock?

PILKINGTON
We'd get a rest.

LONDON
That's right we'd get a... Don't be
absurd. We would get caught.

                    PILKINGTON
I said I was Sorry.

                     LONDON
Yes, well, alright, but do try harder
Pilky. We're nearly home.

                    PILKINGTON
So, what have I missed?

                     LONDON
We've found some Germans having a
picnic and they have a hot air
balloon.

          (Pilkington looks on.)

                    PILKINGTON
So, what's the plan?

                     WINSLOW
Oh, look at all that food.

                    CAVENDISH
Be quiet Winslow.

          *(Winslow trips over a branch
           and falls to the ground.)*

                    GERMAN MAN
Ist jemand da?

LONDON
That's torn it, I guess we'll have to
say something. Look a bit odd if we
just run off...

    *(London walks out of the
    trees and into the open
    field.)*

...Hello there?

    *(The German man gets to his
    feet.)*

GERMAN MAN
Guten Morgen?

    *(London and his men walk
    towards the German couple.)*

LONDON
Lovely day for a stroll, what?

GERMAN MAN
Sprechen Sie Deutsche?

LONDON
Afraid not old bean, learnt the odd
word through watching war films,
Achtung, Hände hoch, Schnell and Ich
habe ein Luger, but other than that
it's a complete mystery.

    (The German man becomes

*agitated by London's words
and motions his wife to stand
behind him. The couple look
scared.)*

GERMAN MAN
Nimm, was du willst, aber bitte töte
uns nicht! (Take what you want, but
please do not kill us!)

*(The German couple put their
hands up and London looks
bewildered.)*

LONDON
Funny behaviour, wonder what's up
with them?

CAVENDISH
You are a plonker London, you've just
told them to put their hands up
because you have a gun.

LONDON
Did I, funny, I thought I was being
amusing. Do you speak German
Cavendish?

CAVENDISH
Aye.

LONDON
Well, tell them everything is alright
and we mean them no harm, there's

been a misunderstanding.

    (Cavendish looks at the
    couple.)

           CAVENDISH
Bitte legen Sie Ihre Hände nieder,
wir meinen Sie nicht schaden. (Please
put your hands down, we mean you no harm.)

    (Winslow runs towards the
    food and starts eating the
    cheese and ham.)

           LONDON
Winslow what are you doing?

           WINSLOW
I can't help it, I'm starving.

    (The German couple become
    alarmed and run towards the
    woods.)

           LONDON
They've run off.

           CAVENDISH
Really?

           CARTER
Seems like they won't be needing that
balloon anymore.

LONDON
Can you fly a balloon carter?

CARTER
There is a first time for everything,
but I know you free the ropes, turn
the gas on and use the thermals to
steer by.

> *(In the woods, the German*
> *couple are shouting to*
> *somebody to come quickly.*
> *Russian soldiers appear in*
> *amongst the pine trees.)*

CARTWRIGHT
The Russian are here!

LONDON
That's blown it. Right, everyone
into the balloon. Winslow, grab the
food.

> *(The sound of AK-47's and ZX-*
> *MF8 tactical rifles rat-a-*
> *tat-tat past London and his*
> *team of ex-SAS soldiers and*
> *they jump into the balloon.*
> *Winslow is the last to climb*
> *aboard.)*

CAVENDISH
Carter, you said you could fly this

thing. Where do we start?

                    CARTER
Put the gas on.

          (Carter moves the gas burner
          and ignites it. The Russian
          soldiers advance quickly
          through the pine forest.)

                    CAVENDISH
Why aren't we moving?

                    CARTER
Give it a minute, the air needs to
warm up...

          (The balloon starts to move,
          but then starts to spin. The
          Russian soldiers are now in
          the clearing and shots whizz
          past them. Cavendish picks
          up his rifle and fires at the
          Russians.)

...There's still one rope attached.

          (Carter runs over to the rope
          still attached to the ground
          and cuts it free. They start
          to rise.)

                    CAVENDISH
Blast, I'm out of bullets.

CARTWRIGHT
Look out! This will give them what
for.

          (Cartwright leans over the
          side of the basket and throws
          a grenade at the advancing
          Russian soldiers. A few
          moments later, the grenade
          explodes and the Russians
          dive for cover. London and
          his men start to cheer as
          they are whisked off into the
          clouds and the hills beyond.
          The Russians cease chasing
          them and shout out colourful
          metaphors and allegory.
          Winslow, overcome with an
          insatiable appetite, sits in
          the corner of the basket
          eating some bread and cheese
          without pause.)

LONDON
Well done Carter, looks like we
needed you after all.

CARTER
Thanks.

Scene fades.

ACT 6, SCENE 3

11.31am. Saturday 18th October, 2025,
Minkov Industrial Estate, Mancho
Oblast, Moscow. On the outskirts of
the city, a truck pulls out of a large
warehouse and disappears down the
road. Inside the warehouse, Alexander
Khrushchev is smoking a cigarette and
walking back towards his office. He
stubs out the cigarette and enters the
main office door and sits down. in
the corner of the room, a T.V. is on.
Katrina Chatovsky from channel 5 news
is reporting.

KATRINA CHATOVSKY
...A 75 year old woman from the town
of Vlogomvich has struck gold after
braking her leg in a yard broom
incident. Reports, although not
totally clear, say the pensioner
slipped on a soda can whilst sweeping
up rubbish in her barn. Apparently,
the floorboards were rotten and she
fell through. During her descent,
her leg struck the bow of a pirate
ship and broke. That's right folks,
a pirate ship. But it wasn't all bad
news for the stumbling pensioner.
When she looked around to get her
bearings, she discovered she had
found a fortune in gold doubloons,
said to be the long lost treasure of
the town's founder, Yagor

Pyritevich...

> *(A car pulls up outside the warehouse and Khrushchev goes to see who it is. As he exits the warehouse, he sees Vadim Schekov walking towards him.)*

                    ALEXANDER KHRUSHCHEV
Oh, it is you. How did everything go?

                    VADIM SCHEKOV
Fine. It is done. They are all dead.

                    ALEXANDER KHRUSHCHEV
Good. Everything seems to be going to plan. I am glad we are rid of those food terrorists and that cosmonaut's wife. I never trusted her, her teeth were too white and her home baked cookies were terrible...

> *(Vadim stares at Khrushchev with disdain and notices some custard and ketchup stains on his shirt.)*

                    VADIM SCHEKOV
I wouldn't know, I never tried them.

> *(Vadim continues to looks at

*Khrushchev and notices his
unpolished shoes and scruffy,
grubby appearance.)*

ALEXANDER SCHEKOV
What do we do now?

VADIM SCHEKOV
The General wants the warehouse burnt
to the ground.

ALEXANDER KHRUSHCHEV
What about the large piece of coal
that was just delivered?

VADIM SCHEKOV
What coal, what are you talking
about?

*(Vadim and Alexander walk
inside. In front of them is
the ovoid shuttlecraft.)*

ALEXANDER KRUSHCHEV
See, a large piece of coal!

*(Vadim walks around the
craft.)*

VADIM SCHEKOV
It is too large for a piece of coal.
Where did it come from?

ALEXANDER KHRUSHCHEV
It came from the Four Seasons hotel
bomb site. General Spuriovsky
ordered it to be delivered here.

(Vadim studies the
shuttlecraft.)

VADIM SCHEKOV
Whatever it is, it is going to be
burnt.

ALEXANDER KHRUSHCHEV
The General was quite excited about
it, he even cancelled next Thursday's
bridge tournament with the crochet
club. Something big must be going
down for him to do that, you know how
much he loves his Bridge...

(Alexander Khrushchev rubs
his hands along the
shuttlecraft.)

...Perhaps he has organised a
barbeque for the troops, a way of
saying thank you for all our hard
work. Do you really think you should
burn it?

VADIM SCHEKOV
I have orders from General Gerasimov
to burn it down and that is what I am
going to do.

*(Vadim walks back to his car
and retrieves some jerry
cans. He walks back inside
the warehouse and starts to
pour petrol over everything.
In the office, the phone
rings and Alexander
Khrushchev answers it.)*

ALEXANDER KHRUSHCHEV
Vadim? It is for you. It is the
General.

VADIM SCHEKOV
Which one?

ALEXANDER KHRUSHCHEV
Gerasimov.

*(Vadim walks into the office
and picks up the phone.)*

VADIM SCHEKOV
Yes.

GENERAL GERASIMOV
They have escaped.

VADIM SCHEKOV
Who?

GENERAL GERASIMOV
Dmitry and Yuri.

                    VADIM SCHEKOV
How is that possible?

                  GENERAL GERASIMOV
The how doesn't matter. Find them
and kill them.

                    VADIM SCHEKOV
Do you know where they went?

                  GERNERAL GERASIMOV
The last report says they stole a
light blue campervan and were heading
towards Moscow. That is all I know.
I am leaving for Moscow now, meet me
in the Red Square. Whatever happens,
we can't let them get to the News
Station. We must stop them.
Remember Vadim, no loose ends!

                    VADIM SCHEKOV
Yes, I remember. Leave it to me.

          (Vadim puts the phone down.
          He continues to pour petrol
          over everything in the
          office. When the cans are
          empty he throws a lit lighter
          onto a pile of papers and
          walks outside with Alexander.
          The warehouse starts to
          burn.)

ALEXANDER KHRUSHCHEV
What do you what me to tell General
Spuriovsky?

VADIM SCHEKOV
Nothing.

(Vadim takes out a gun and
shoots Khrushchev in the
chest.)

ALEXANDER KHRUSHCHEV
Why did you do that?

VADIM SCHEKOV
Because you know too much...

(Vadim stands over
Khrushchev.)

...And I don't like loose ends!

(Vadim shoots Khrushchev in
the head.)

Scene fades.

ACT 6, SCENE 4

11.37am. Saturday 18th October, 2025.
Dmitry, Yuri and the Moon Man arrive
at a small rural village called Miklo,
15 miles outside Moscow city centre.
They pull into a parking lot with a
general store, a bus stop, an old
cigarette vending machine, recycling
bins and a payphone.   The 1971
Volkswagen caravanette is spraying out
steam from the rear of the vehicle and
is moving erratically.

                    DMITRY
The engine is overheating, we need
water. I better stop her quickly, or
she will blow up.

                    YURI
There is a space available over
there.

        (Yuri points to an empty
        space next to some recycling
        bins. Dmitry turns off the
        engine and rolls the final
        few yards into the parking
        space and stops. He looks
        around anxiously.)

                    DMITRY
We need to get out of these orange
jump suits and find some real clothes

and we need money.

                    YURI
How are we going to do that?

                  MOON MAN
We could put on a show if we had some
costumes, I'm really good at lip
syncing to Y.M.C.A by the *Village
People.*

                   DMITRY
That is a stupid idea, we need real
solutions to our problems, not
flights of fancy. How can we get
costumes if we can't even get
clothes?

                  MOON MAN
Well excuse me for thinking outside
the box, I was only trying to help.
If you want some different clothes,
why don't you try those recycling
bins over there, it looks like one of
them is a Salvation Army container.

          *(Dmitry and Yuri look across
          the parking lot at the
          Salvation Army clothes
          recycling bin.)*

                   DMITRY
Now that is a good suggestion...

(Dmitry looks at his and
Yuri's clothes and then at
the Moon Man's.)

...You better go over there and grab
something for us, we are too, too...

MOON MAN
...Orange.

DMITRY
Exactly, we are too orange.

(The Moon Man takes off his
broken crescent moon and
removes his one remaining
shoe and trots over to the
clothes recycling bins. He
takes out two black bags and
scampers back to the camper.)

MOON MAN
These are really heavy, there should
be some good stuff in here.

(Dmitry, Yuri and the Moon
Man start looking through the
bags. Dmitry looks at the
Moon Man.)

DMITRY
You better take some of this stuff
and change your clothes as well, you
won't get very far looking like that.

MOON MAN
Like what?

DMITRY
Y'know, like a drag queen.

MOON MAN
A drag queen, is that what you think
I look like? My mother and my auntie
made this costume for the Mooncalf
Festival, it's a work of art. It
should be on show at *The Russian
Clothes and Textiles Museum* in Moscow
as a piece of modern inspiration for
all the world to see.

YURI
I don't think Dmitry meant any
offence, it just makes sense that you
change the way you look. General
Gerasimov will be looking for two
orange men and a crescent moon. The
further away from looking like this
we can get, the better for all of us.

MOON MAN
Oh yes, I see...

            (*The Moon Man pulls out an
            item of clothing from one of
            the black bags.*)

...Oh, this is nice, pale blue satin.
I just love pale blue, it matches my

eyes. Oh, and look at the trumpet
halter. It must have been someone's
Prom dress. It's simply divine. I
must try this on.

                    DMITRY
Perhaps you should try something
else...

          (Dmitry pulls out a pair of
          tweed trousers, a parker
          jacket and some white
          trainers.)

...Put these on.

                    MOON MAN
These are awful, not the sort of
thing I would wear, I mean who would?

                    DMITRY
Listen, we are trying to keep a low
profile. That means we need to wear
plain clothes and keep our
gesticulations to a minimum.

                    MOON MAN
Sounds boring to me, where's the fun
in that?

                    DMITRY
There is none. We are trying to stay
alive, not enter a beauty pageant.

                    MOON MAN
Well, when you put it like that...

        (The Moon Man looks at the
        items.)

...I suppose we might be able to do
something with this. Do either of
you have a pair of scissors and some
pink thread?

                    DMITRY
What, are you crazy? Just put on the
items, and lose that stupid Dolly
Parton wig.

                    MOON MAN
Oh, no, not my wig; and it's not
Dolly Parton, it's Farrah Fawcett.
Before she went off with that Major's
guy.

        (Yuri pulls out a brown and
        beige shell suit from the bag
        and puts it on, along with
        some grey sandals. Dmitry
        finds some plaid trousers, a
        ruffled lavender coloured
        shirt, a yellow and silver
        blazer and light brown
        espadrilles.)

                    DMITRY
I don't suppose we will win any

fashion contests, but we have clothes. Now, we need money, any suggestions?

                    MOON MAN
I have an idea?

                    DMITRY
I am afraid to ask. What is it?

                    MOON MAN
We could check all of the pockets in the clothes we just got. Somebody may have left some change inside.

                    DMITRY
That is another great idea...

          (They start to search the
          pockets of the new clothes
          and Yuri finds just over 800
          Rubles, Dmitry finds 40
          Kopeck and the Moon Man finds
          some buttons and a hair
          clip.)

...Eight hundred and forty Rubles, not a bad haul. Right, I am going to use that payphone over there and contact the Penachy County Jail and tell them they have a bomb threat. Then I will phone the channel Five News Station and tell them our little tale. When I return we will look for

some water for the camper and see if
we can find your bear. While I am
gone, see if you can get something
for us to eat and drink from that
shop over there.

                    YURI
Do you think the News Station will
believe you Dmitry?

                  DMITRY
I don't know, but we have to try.

          (Dmitry gets out of the
          camper and walks over to the
          payphone. Yuri opens his
          door and looks back at the
          Moon Man.)

                    YURI
Wait here, I won't be long.

          (Yuri closes the door and
          walks to the general store.
          Inside the store, behind the
          checkout counter, channel 5
          News is showing on a T.V.
          The story is covering the
          explosion at the Penachy
          County Jail. Anastasia
          Bedlumvich is reporting from
          the scene. Pictures of the
          devastation are being shown
          as the camera follows her

while she walks amongst the
wreckage.)

ANASTASIA BEDLUMVICH
...Here, at the Penachy County
Jailhouse, you can see the
devastation of yet another bombing
that has all the earmarks of the
O.F.E. How many are dead is yet
unknown, but it is believed Prime
Minister Kantcoughsky, three police
officers and two unidentified bodies
have been found so far. As you know,
last night, Viktor Popov and
Alexander Ivanov escaped from the
Butrayka prison, killing two guards
and a hedge hog in the process.
During their escape, they attacked a
55 year old ice cream vender, stole
his wagon and used it as a getaway
vehicle. Only an hour ago, police
discovered that same ice cream wagon
just two blocks from the Penachy
County Jailhouse. This discovery has
led the police to believe that Viktor
Popov and Alexander Ivanov are
responsible for today's bombing.
They have also stated that they
believe the bombings are connected to
Prime Minister Kantcoughsky and that
he has been the intended target for
the recent bombings. A manhunt
started today to catch the two
escaped prisoners and an 800,000
rubles rewards has been offered to

anyone helping to bring them to justice. This is Anastasia Bedlumvich reporting for channel 5 News...

> *(Inside the general store, Yuri hurries to buy some food and supplies. At the checkout he notices 'The Moscow Enquirer' on a magazine rack. On the cover is Miss Decapinovsky, a girl scout and a tartan teddy bear - the tag line reads: 'Ghost of Russian Cosmonauts seen at Hotel Bombing'. He takes one and adds it to his shopping. He heads back to the camper and finds Dmitry pouring water from a green watering can into the radiator.)*

YURI
Where did you get the water from?

DMITRY
There is a pet cemetery just behind that wall, they keep water there for the flowers people bring.

YURI
A pet cemetery, that is nice. Dmitry, The Jail has been blown up?

(Dmitry continues to pour water into the radiator.)

DMITRY
Yes, I know. When I phoned the number, they put me through to some crisis centre. That Vadim sure does work fast...

(Dmitry puts down the watering can, tightens the cap on the radiator and wipes his hands.)

...How did you find out about the jail?

YURI
I saw the news in the shop, they are blaming Viktor and Alexander for the bombing. There was a fake story about them escaping from Butrayka prison last night.

DMITRY
That doesn't surprise me. It is just as well we are dead or they would be reporting rubbish about us.

YURI
I am afraid that hasn't stopped them...

(Yuri pulls out 'The Moscow

*Enquirer' from his bag and
hands it to Dmitry.)*

...Take a look at this.

*(Dmitry reads the front
page.)*

DMITRY
That woman's crazy, why would we be
ghosts?..

(Dmitry continues to read.)

...There is the little girl with your
bear...

(Dmitry scans the page.)

...Story continued on page 7...

*(Dmitry fans to page seven
and begins to study the
page.)*

...Listen to this Yuri. It says
here, there is going to be the Annual
Girl Scouts Parade in the Red Square
on Saturday 18th October at 1pm as
part of the Moscow *Vodka and Soft
Drink Autumn Festival*...

(Dmitry looks at Yuri.)

Why, that's today!...

(Dmitry looks around to find
a clock tower and sees one in
the distance.)

...11.52. There's just over an hour
before the parade starts. We better
get going.

YURI
But do you think she will have my
bear?

(Dmitry shows Yuri the
article.)

DMITRY
Look at this picture. See how
tightly she is holding your bear, she
loves it, and don't forget Yuri, it
was given to her by the ghost of a
Russian cosmonaut...

(Dmitry hands Yuri the
magazine, picks up the
watering can and throws it
over the wall.)

...C'mon Yuri we don't have much
time.

(Dmitry gets into the
driver's seat and starts the
camper and puts the heater
on. Yuri gets into the

*passenger seat and closes his
door.)*

                    YURI
Oh, you never told me how you fared
with the News Station?

                    DMITRY
It was just like you said. They
thought I was a crackpot. The more I
tried to explain the worse it got.
The woman on the other end of the
phone wouldn't listen to me and said
the call was in bad taste. After a
few minutes, she transferred me to a
mental health counselling service.
At that point I hung up.

                    YURI
That's too bad. We need to get a
hold of that Anastasia Bedlumvich, I
bet she would listen to what we have
to say if we saw her face to face.

                    DMITRY
You think so?

          *(Dmitry raises his eyebrows
          and rolls his eyes.)*

                    YURI
Sure. She seems like a real go-
getter.

(*The Moon Man pulls on the back of Dmitry's seat and leans forward.*)

MOON MAN
So, what's happening now?

DMITRY
We are going to the *Vodka and Soft Drink Autumn Festival* in Moscow.

MOON MAN
What, dressed like this?

DMITRY
You don't have to come, it is probably best if you stay here and wait for a bus. At least you are safe now. We don't know what's going to happen in Moscow, General Gerasimov could be looking for us along with his henchmen. It could get bad for all of us.

MOON MAN
You can't leave me here waiting for a bus, they only run on Mondays and Wednesdays. I can't sit here for two days lurking around like some degenerate ragamuffin...

(*The Moon Man clings to Dmitry's shoulder.*)

...Y'know me, I get bored easily.
Before long, someone's bound to fall
over my big feet and blame me. Don't
leave me here, I'd rather stay with
you two and see it through to the
end.

          (Dmitry removes the Moon
          Man's tight fingers from his
          shoulder and looks at him.)

               DMITRY
Okay, but it might be the end for all
of us...

          (The Moon Man smiles and sits
          back. Dmitry puts the camper
          in gear and they pull away.)

...Imagine, a bus service that only
runs two days a week? Things are
worse than I thought.

               YURI
You can blame Kantcoughsky for that.
That was one of his initiatives to
save money and decrease pollution.

               DMITRY
That sounds like one of his ideas,
the snake.

               YURI
Oh, I forgot to tell you, he is dead.

                    DMITRY
Who?

                    YURI
Kantcoughsky. He died in the
bombing.

                    DMITRY
At least something good has come out
of this day...

        (Dmitry smiles then looks
        sad.)

...What about Olga?

                    YURI
They didn't mention her name.

                    DMITRY
Pity.

        (Dmitry drops down a gear and
        speeds off.)

Scene fades.

ACT 6, SCENE 5

12.38pm. Saturday 18th October, 2025. London and his group of ex-SAS soldiers have been flying around for over an hour and have lost all sense of direction. Inside the basket, London struggles to read his map and adequately seek out a landmark. Winslow has eaten too much food and has a stomach ache and Cartwright is suffering from altitude sickness. Carter and Cavendish are fighting over the gas lever and Pilkington is sitting in a corner of the basket. Around them, small towns drift by as they head over buildings and begin to leave the countryside far behind.

CARTER
Look, stop pulling on that gas lever, we're going too high, I want to stay in this thermal, it's going the right way.

CAVENDISH
I don't think you know what you're doing Carter we've been drifting north-east for the past hour, we're supposed to be going west towards Dry Oakov.

CARTER
What do you want to go there for,

it's in the middle of nowhere?

                    CAVENDISH
I thought that were plan.

                     CARTER
All I know is we've found
civilisation and that's a good thing.

        *(London walks over to Carter
        holding his map.)*

                     LONDON
Finally made some sense of this
thing. Looks like you've been going
north-east for the last hour. If my
calculations are correct, we are only
ten minutes outside Moscow. Don't
know if that's exactly where we want
to go, bit populated...

        *(London shows Carter the
        map.)*

...See this place here Carter called
Miklo, I've got a contact there from
the old days. If we start our
descent now we should be on it in the
next couple of minutes.

        *(Cavendish puts his hands
        back on the gas lever and
        Carter turns to face him.)*

CARTER
Will you stop tugging on this lever,
you'll break the thing in a minute...

        (Carter pulls the lever away
        from Cavendish and it snaps.
        The balloon starts to rise.)

...Now look what you've done.

        (The balloon starts to rise
        quickly and becomes unstable
        in a high crosswind.
        London's map is whipped from
        his hands suddenly and he
        grabs the basket to save
        going with it.)

LONDON
Blast, lost the map! Look, there's
Miklo, that's our stop!

CARTWRIGHT
I wish somebody would make it stop, I
don't feel so well.

CARTER
That's torn it, the gas is stuck on
full.

PILKINGTON
Perhaps you can blow it out.

                    LONDON
Need a good bit of puff for that
Pilky, I think we need a better plan
than that. I'm sure there must be a
stop valve or vent around here
somewhere to release the hot air.

                  CAVENDISH
We better do something quick, if we
keep going up at this rate it's going
to get really cold.

                    LONDON
Isn't there a vent on this thing
somewhere Carter?

                    CARTER
Yes, but the ropes been shot and I
can't reach it.

                  CAVENDISH
Someone will have to go up and get
it.

                    LONDON
Seems a bit tricky. You'd have to
climb on the outside and cut your way
in. Can't you just turn the gas off?

                    CARTER
I tried that, its damaged and the
valve won't close.

                    LONDON
Well, can't you just cut the pipe?

                    CAVENDISH
Don't be so bleeding stupid. If you
cut the gas pipe, you'll blow us all
up.

                    LONDON
Ah, yes, never thought of that.
Well, I guess someone is going to
have to climb up there and make a
hole...

     (London looks at carter.)

Carter, up you go, there's a good
fellow.

                    CARTER
Why me, why doesn't Cavendish do it?
He got us into this mess.

                    LONDON
Cavendish is a bit bulky for that
sort of thing, and besides you have
the knife. Now, there's a good chap,
up you go...

          *(Carter takes out his knife
          and puts it between his
          teeth, grabs hold of the
          outer rope and pulls himself
          onto the net of the balloon*

and starts to climb.)

...You'll have to go all the way to the top and cut open the deflation vent.

                    CARTER
Why didn't I think of that.

        *(Carter climbs up the side of
        the balloon. The cold air
        batters his face and the task
        becomes painful. The balloon
        continues to rise and London
        and Cavendish watch Carter's
        movements with great concern
        and unease.)*

                    LONDON
Carter's not such a bad sort after all, bit of a complainer and a slacker, but in the last couple of hours he has shown a resolve and fortitude I never thought he had in him. That's the true British spirit climbing up that rope Cavendish, that's the sort of true grit that made the empire great...

        *(Carter continues to climb up
        the rope as the balloon sways
        violently in the icy wind.
        He loses his grip and bounces
        from the side of the balloon
        but manages to grab a rope.)*

...Good heavens, thought he was a
gonna that time.

>   (Carter grabs the net and
>   begins climbing again. He
>   looks in trouble and his
>   motions are slow.)

                    CAVENDISH
C'mon Carter, you can do it.

>   (Winslow emerges from his
>   food pile and Pilkington and
>   Cartwright walk over to the
>   edge of the basket and begin
>   to shout words of
>   encouragement to Carter.)

                    PILKINGTON
Go on Carter, you can do it.

                    CARTWRIGHT
That's it Carter, you're nearly
there!

>   (Winslow is still chewing on
>   a piece of Pumpernickel and
>   is oblivious to their current
>   dilemma. He staggers over to
>   Cartwright and offers him
>   some bread.)

WINSLOW
What's happening, it's getting a bit
chilly?

CARTWRIGHT
Carter's gone up top to free the
vent, it's stuck and we can't
descend.

WINSLOW
I thought we were getting a bit high.

*(Winslow walks back to his
food pile and covers himself
with the picnic blanket. Out
on the balloon, Carter has
reached the top. He takes
the knife from his mouth and
rips the balloon material.
Hot air gushes onto his face
and he feels relief from the
cold. Everyone in the
basket, except Winslow starts
to cheer. The balloon begins
to descend.)*

LONDON
Great job Carter, you can come down
now...

*(Carter warms his hands over
the new hole then starts to
climb down. London turns to
Cavendish.)*

...Well Cavendish, seem to be
descending nicely.

(Cartwright shouts out.)

                CARTWRIGHT
Look! that's the Red Square.

*(London and Cavendish move
over to the other side of the
balloon.)*

                LONDON
Looks like you're right Cartwright.
Still a bit off in the distance.

*(Carter climbs into the
wicker basket.)*

                CARTER
That was harder than it looked.

                LONDON
Well done Carter, you've saved the
day...

*(The wind picks up and blows
the balloon violently. The
rip in the top gets much
bigger and the rate of
descent increases
dramatically.)*

...Cripes, hold on everyone.

                    (A strong tail wind starts to
                    push them towards Moscow and
                    they start to fall.)

                    PILKINGTON
We are going down too fast.

                    CAVENDISH
Throw the sand bags over, they're
pulling us down.

                    (Everyone starts to untie the
                    sand bags and let them go.)

                    LONDON
Hope they don't land on anyone's
head.

                    (The balloon slows its rate
                    of descent.)

                    PILKINGTON
I don't think we're falling as fast.

                    LONDON
Still seems a bit fierce to me.
Looks like we're going to end up in
Moscow. It's out of our hands now.
Should be arriving in about 15
minutes time I'd say if this tail
wind keeps up.

CARTER
What did I tell you. I bet you
anything you like we end up at the
train station.

LONDON
The train's not an option Carter, you
should know that. We can't travel
without a passport, not to dear old
Blighty at any rate.

CARTER
Then what are we gonna do?

LONDON
Nothing's changed Carter. I'll
contact HQ when we land and arrange a
pick up. Can't see them refusing to
collect us now, not when we have
Winslow's magic crystals and your
splendid gold medallion. I imagine
they'll pull out the red carpet and
crack open the champagne and send us
home first class all the way.

CAVENDISH
We've got to get out of this balloon
first and avoid the Russian
authorities before that can happen.

LONDON
You're always so negative Cavendish,
haven't I got us this far? All we
have to do is lay low for a few hours

in a coffee house or wine bar until
our transport arrives. I don't
foresee any problems, stop being such
a blighter Cavendish, it's not
becoming.

                    CARTWRIGHT
Hear, hear! Well said.

                    CAVENDISH
Well, if you feel that way about it,
I won't say another word...

          *(Winslow gets up from his
          seated position and puts his
          head over the side. He
          starts to throw up but it
          blows back towards Cavendish
          and gets him in the face.)*

...Oh, you mucky twerp, watch what
you're doing will yeh. You got me
right in the face.

                    LONDON
That's the ticket Winslow, good show.
You know what they always say?

          *(Cavendish wipes his face
          with a napkin from the picnic
          basket.)*

                    WINSLOW
No, what do they always say?

LONDON
Better out than in...

(*London smiles at Cavendish
and looks towards Moscow and
pats Winslow on the back.*)

...Quite invigorating this breeze,
makes you feel alive. Have to say
though, also gives you a fierce
appetite. Mind you, with any luck,
there'll be a nice tea shop in the
old Red Square where I can get a cup
of Darjeeling and a Pikelet.

WINSLOW
I'm not hungry anymore, just queasy.

LONDON
What you need is a nice ginger
flavoured boiled sweet to suck on,
that will put you back on top. Bound
to be a purveyor of fine sugar
confection in Moscow with it being
the capital and all.

Scene fades.

ACT 6, SCENE 6

12.51pm. Saturday 18th October, 2025. Dmitry, Yuri and the Moon Man have arrived in Moscow and are stuck in a traffic jam. The streets are alive with people and the festival is in full swing. Floats with fabulous designs move slowly down the street as music is pumped out through a loud speaker system. People dressed in colourful costumes of flamingos, peacocks, rainbows, parrots and toucans dance down the street singing along with the music. Anti-colour protestors stand at the sidelines dressed in black and white outfits - Nuns, policemen, French maids, prisoners, sailors and judges all wave banners of objection as they walk by. Large balloons of cars, buildings, pigs, spaceships, aeroplanes and helicopters fly high above the street blowing in the breeze. In the centre of the Red Square, military personal move about the crowds giving orders. In the distance, an armed unit of tanks, jeeps and trucks drive through the busy streets. General Gerasimov leads the convoy. Tents of all shapes and sizes filled with merchandise ranging from tarot cards to teddy bears line the Red Square's outer edges. Vendors cry out in the noise to boast their wares.

DMITRY

This is utter chaos, we are never
going to get through this crowd. We
are jammed in here like sardines in a
tin. There doesn't seem to be
anywhere to park.

MOON MAN

Don't it look wonderful. I always
wanted to go to the Autumn Festival
in Moscow.

DMITRY

It is good you have realised a dream,
but can you keep an eye open for a
parking place.

MOON MAN

Oh, how can you concern yourself with
such a mundane thing as a parking
place when you have all of this for
your eyes to feast on, such gaiety,
exuberance and colour to behold. I
am in awe, and you keep going on
about a parking place, you're ruining
the whole experience.

> *(A dark blue van pulls into
> the traffic and creates a
> parking place for Dmitry.)*

YURI

Dmitry, quick! That van has made a
space for you to park.

*(Dmitry pulls into the space
and parks.)*

DMITRY
C'mon Yuri, we don't have much time.

*(Dmitry and Yuri open the
camper's doors to leave.)*

MOON MAN
What about me?

DMITRY
You can do whatever you want. You
are in Moscow and you are safe.
You're on your own. I would like to
say it was nice knowing you, but I
would be lying.

MOON MAN
So, that's it?

*(Yuri opens the camper door
and gets out. He looks back
at the Moon Man who is
fumbling with a
handkerchief.)*

YURI
I am sorry, but everything ends.
Send us a postcard and let us know
how you are doing.

MOON MAN
Send you a postcard? I thought we
were friends?

(Yuri hands the Moon Man some
loose change.)

YURI
Here, get yourself an ice cream and
watch the parade.

(The Moon Man wipes his eyes
with his handkerchief and
looks down at the money.)

MOON MAN
50 kopeck, what a cheek! I won't
even get a cone with that, and I'll
have to have plain vanilla.

YURI
I'm sorry, that's all I have spare.

DMITRY
C'mon Yuri, we don't have much time.

(Dmitry pulls Yuri away from
the Moon Man and they start
to run along the street.
Before long, they are caught
up in a sea of people and can
hardly move.)

                    YURI
This is impossible, I am getting
squashed by a large cheese.

                    DMITRY
Just keep moving...

        *(People in various states of
        drunkenness continue to
        hinder their movements:
        clowns, jugglers, jesters,
        knife throwers with portable
        dartboards and ladies on
        stilts block up the pavement
        and the street.)*

...This is crazy!

        *(A float full of jazz
        musicians and flamingos joins
        the parade and the crowd
        follows them down the street
        away from the Red Square and
        the main thoroughfare.)*

                    YURI
Head towards those tents Dmitry, I
see a space in the crowd...

        *(Dmitry and Yuri lose the
        crowd and arrive at a tent
        selling teddy bears and gold
        fish. Yuri speaks to the
        vendor.)*

...How much for one of those bears?

                    VENDOR
200 Rubles.

                     YURI
Good, pass me the one with the yellow
tartan trousers.

        *(The vendor hands over the
        bear and Yuri counts out the
        last of his money.)*

                    DMITRY
What do you want with that bear?

                     YURI
When we find the little girl, we
can't just steal her bear, but we can
replace it with another...

        (Yuri shows Dmitry the bear.)

...This one is pretty close to my
Rupertvich and if we swap it quickly
and make our escape, no one will
realise until later. At which point
we will be ourselves again.

                    DMITRY
That is good thinking Yuri, the last
thing we need is an hysterical child
moaning about her teddy being stolen
by two strange men.

*(Dmitry and Yuri run down a
line of tents looking for one
belonging to the Girl Scouts.
After a quick search, they
arrive at a tent marked with
a cardboard cut-out of a full
sized Girl Scout with three
middle fingers raised and the
slogan - 'Serving up our
people, one person at a
time.')*

                    YURI
Dmitry, look! We are here. This is
tent for Girl Scouts.

          *(Dmitry looks at the
          cardboard cut-out.)*

                    DMITRY
Either their slogan has been worded
badly or the Girl Scouts have found a
way to solve the nation's food
crisis.

          *(Dmitry and Yuri walk into
          the tent. Inside, parents
          are helping their children
          with marching and smiling
          techniques for the parade and
          making minor adjustments to
          the cut of the girls
          uniforms.   The tent is
          decorated with wind chimes,
          cloves of garlic, dream*

*catchers, sprigs of lavender
and horseshoes. Incense
burners are scattered
throughout the tent wafting
the sweet smell of sage and
asafoetida and tea lights
heat patchouli oil candle
blocks. On the floor, a
circle of salt runs around
the edge of the tent. In the
corner, the little girl Yuri
and Dmitry are looking for is
talking to her mother and
Miss Decapinovsky. She is
holding Yuri's bear in her
left hand.)*

DMITRY
Yuri, there is the girl; and she has
your bear.

MISS DECAPINOVSKY
Listen up everyone. Two minutes and
we start making our way to the
square. Remember to keep those heads
up and those smiles wide...

*(Dmitry and Yuri walk over to
Miss Decapinovsky and the
young girl. Miss
Decapinovsky sees Yuri and
Dmitry walking towards her.)*

...Ghosts! It's the ghosts of Yuri
Chekov and Dmitry Usakov. I told you

they'd come back. Look! They have
entered the circle of salt, they must
be powerful demons.   Wooaahhh!

> *(Miss Decapinovsky runs out
> of the tent. The tent goes
> quiet and everyone is focused
> on Dmitry and Yuri.)*

                DMITRY
Stupid woman. How is she in charge
of little children, she is mad. She
is insane...

> *(Dmitry puts his hands up in
> the air and waves them
> about.)*

...No need to panic, we have just
come for the girl with the bear.

                GIRL SCOUT'S MOTHER
Stay away spectre...

> *(The woman grabs a broom and
> starts waving it in front of
> Dmitry while shielding her
> child.)*

...Be gone from this place and return
to where you came from.

                DMITRY
They are all mad.

YURI
Dmitry, you are scaring them...

(Yuri walks forward.)

...Listen? We have not come to hurt
anyone. We just need the little
tartan bear the girl in the corner
has and we will be on our way. We
have another bear to give her, just
as nice...

(Yuri holds up the bear.)

...See, we mean you no harm.

GIRL SCOUT'S MOTHER
Stay where you are spirit, or I will
let you have it with this broom.
Miss Decapinovsky said you might come
back, and she was right. Now, be
gone with you, and return from whence
you came.

DMITRY
Don't be so stupid. If we were
really spirits, that broom head would
just go straight through us.

GIRL SCOUT'S MOTHER
Let's see shall we.

(The woman lunges forward and
hits Dmitry with the broom.

*The broom snaps. Miss
Decapinovsky returns with a
fire extinguisher and fires
it at Dmitry and Yuri. They
are covered in white foam
along with half the tent.)*

                    YURI
Dmitry, I can't see.

                    DMITRY
Hold on...

*(In the chaos, Dmitry grabs
Yuri's bear from the little
girl and takes Yuri's hand
and leads him out of the
tent. The young girl starts
to scream and the mother and
miss Decapinovsky start to
follow. Yuri drops his
replacement bear in the mud.)*

...Run for it Yuri!

*(Yuri wipes his eyes and they
run from the screaming
madness of the Girl Scout
tent. They hide behind an
army truck and duck down
behind a wheel to catch their
breath. From their position,
they can see lots of legs
moving quickly and then the
face of Miss Decapinovsky as*

*she looks under various
vehicles. A few of the other
mothers walk past them and
they remain very still.)*

MISS DECAPINOVSKY
The demons are gone! They must have
returned to their realm. Quick,
everyone back to the children, we
have a show to put on.

*(Miss Decapinovsky and the
mothers return to their
tent.)*

YURI
That could have gone better, but at
least we have bear. Is the card
there Dmitry?

DMITRY
Let me see...

*(Dmitry rummages around
inside the bear's stomach and
pulls out the card.)*

...It is here.

YURI
Good. Now, let's get out of here and
get to a News Station...

(Dmitry and Yuri wipe off

*most off their foam suit and
step out from behind the army
truck only for Dmitry to push
Yuri back out of sight.)*

...What is Wrong?

                    DMITRY
General Gerasimov and two armed
soldiers are coming this way.

                     YURI
What will we do?

                    DMITRY
Let me think.

          *(The voice of the General can
          be heard from where they
          are.)*

              GENERAL GERASIMOV
They must be around here somewhere,
their blue campervan has just been
found by F-squad. You two take the
parade tents and search them. Report
back to me in 30 minutes.

                    DMITRY
I guess we won't be returning to our
stolen vehicle.

                    YURI
I hope the Moon Man was not inside.

                    DMITRY
I thought you didn't like that guy?

                    YURI
He was a bit odd for sure, but I
wouldn't want any harm to come to
him. How do you think General
Gerasimov got to Moscow so quick?

                    DMITRY
Knowing him, he probably has a tunnel
with a monorail system leading
straight to the city.

                    YURI
Do you really think so?

                    DMITRY
No, he probably came in one of the
helicopters over there...

          (Dmitry points to some
          helicopters parked in the
          centre of the square.)

...C'mon, the coast is clear.

Scene fades.

ACT 6, SCENE 7

On board the starship Red Neval, KAL takes the hyperdrive off line and restores normal cruising speed of 50,000 miles an hour. MacTavish is still asleep in his chair, oblivious to the change in speed and everything else. Moments later, an alarm sounds and KAL starts to crank a large brass flywheel with his right hand whilst pumping a pair of copper bellows with his left foot. The noise level in the bridge continues to increase and MacTavish wakes up.

MACTAVISH
Fit's goin' on, fits all the noise aboot, my head's comin' aff!

(KAL dances around the bridge controls pushing buttons and pulling levers.)

KAL
Ah, good, you're awake. Come over here, I need your assistance.

(MacTavish gets up from his chair and staggers over to KAL.)

MACTAVISH
Could ye call that alarm aff, I've

got my own bells in ma head!

                    KAL

Yes, of course.

        (*KAL pushes a button and the
        alarm stops.*)

                  MACTAVISH

That's better. My lugs were on
overload. Now, fit would ye like me
tae do?

                    KAL

When I say Now, I want you to pull
that big lever towards you and lock
it in place.

                  MACTAVISH

This lever with the big red knob?

        (*MacTavish points at a big
        tall lever with a red knob on
        the top.*)

                    KAL

Yes, that's the one. Get ready -
NOW!

        (*KAL moves quickly around the
        controls and MacTavish pulls
        the lever. The ship slows
        down and out of the window
        Earth comes into view.*)

                    MACTAVISH
Is that Earth?

                      KAL
Yes, we are here. According to my
calculations, the Medallion of Life
is currently on the move and flying
over a city called Moscow.

                    MACTAVISH
Did you say flying over?

                      KAL
Yes. For some reason it seems to be
floating in the sky. It's the oddest
thing...

     *(KAL stares at his
     instruments.)*

...I suppose the best thing to do is
go and have a look...

     *(KAL pushes some buttons and
     levers and the ship heads
     towards Earth.)*

...Moscow here we come!

                    MACTAVISH
I hope the Earthlings look a wee
bitty like us and nae like strange
monsters with tentacles 'n' antennas.

KAL
I believe they have most of the same
attributes as us except they have an
extra finger on each hand, small
beady eyes and a flat head.

MACTAVISH
Wee eyes, a flat head and an extra
finger?

KAL
Yes, that's right.

MACTAVISH
I could aye use an extra finger, bit
wee eyes? I dinnae trust anybody
with wee eyes.

KAL
Well, we don't need to trust anyone.
We are actually here to take the
Medallion of Life away from someone,
so we are technically stealing it.

MACTAVISH
I did a wee bit o' pickpocketing when
I was wee, but nothing serious.

KAL
Glad to here it...

     (KAL pulls some levers and
     the ship slows.)

...We are entering Earth's
atmosphere. The gravity pull seems
quite fierce, didn't expect that.

(*The alarm starts to sound
off again.*)

SHIP'S COMPUTER
Warning, rate of descent too steep.
Please adjust pitch and speed.
Horizontal stabilisers are failing.
Deploying emergency parachute to
correct pitch and angle of descent.

MACTAVISH
Fit's happening?

KAL
Looks like we are losing hull
integrity throughout the ship and we
are coming in too fast. Better press
the time delay button.

MACTAVISH
Time delay button, fit's that do?

KAL
It pauses time for a moment and
allows us to carry out important
tasks like reinitializing the
horizontal stabilisers.

                    MACTAVISH
Pauses time? That's impossible!

          *(KAL pushes some buttons and
          walks over to a large handle
          and starts to crank it.)*

                      KAL
I assure you it's not...

          *(KAL builds up the speed on
          the crank and the ship's
          lights get brighter. A ting
          noise is heard followed by a
          whizz. In front of him, a
          circular board appears with
          various time slots printed on
          it. The board spins round.)*

...It's stopping.

          *(A ta-da sound is heard and a
          time appears on the board.
          The ship's computer speaks.)*

                 SHIP'S COMPUTER
You have been awarded seven minutes
of free time.

                      KAL
Seven minutes? We'll have to work
fast...

          *(Outside, the spaceship hangs

*in the clouds like a
stationary object. Time has
stopped for KAL and
MacTavish.)*

...MacTavish, I'm going to need you
to reinitialise the horizontal
stabilisers when I engage the forward
brake. Unfortunately, it's stuck in
manual mode, so I am going to have to
go outside and activate them
manually. If I'm not back in seven
minutes, brace for impact.

                MACTAVISH
Fit do ye mean ye are goin' outdoors?

                  KAL
It's the only way I'm afraid. Don't
have time to explain. Just get ready
with that stabiliser lever.

        *(KAL leaves the bridge and
        MacTavish looks at the bridge
        control panel and talks to
        himself.)*

                MACTAVISH
Fit one did he say was the
stabilising lever again? I dinnae
remember him telling me.

Scene fades.

ACT 6, SCENE 8

1.04pm. Saturday 18th October, 2025.
London and his group of ex-SAS
soldiers are throwing everything they
can out of the basket. The gas has
run out and the balloon is falling
fast. The men now find themselves
over Moscow city heading for the Red
Square.

                PILKINGTON
I don't like this at all.

                 LONDON
Don't just stand there panicking
Pilky, find something to throw out.

                PILKINGTON
There's nothing left, it's all gone.

                 LONDON
This is it chaps, brace for impact.

          (The men cling to the basket
          as the balloon sails over the
          buildings and into the Red
          Square. They are about to
          hit the ground when they get
          a sudden boost from a
          helicopter which is getting
          ready for takeoff. They
          start to move horizontally
          and slide along the ground

heading towards some army trucks and parade tents. In the square, the Girl Scouts are marching and smiling and singing a traditional Scouts motto song.)

GIRL SCOUTS
...Ra, ra, ra. Ra, ra, ra. Ra, ra, ra.

Fid-il-die plop, fid-il-die plop, fid-il-die pooh.

We are the Girl Scouts of Moscow

Our knowledge to you we bestow.

Show you how to shoot a gun

Or how to bake a bun

For you, we'll put on a show.

Hay, hay, hay, hoe, hoe, hoe

We are the Girl Scouts of Moscow

....

Tell you how to light a fire,

skin a rabbit or a bear,

make a Molotov Cocktail

from some vodka you have spare...

(With a final gust of wind, the balloon, with its basket, rises up into the air over the heads of the Girl Scouts and hangs momentarily in space.)

WINSLOW
I'm going to be sick again.

*(At one of the parade stands,
Dmitry and Yuri browse over a
selection of Dream Catchers
and Tarot Cards.)*

YURI

My great aunt Galina use to read palm
and tell fortune. She even had ball
that told future.

DMITRY

Really? I think that stuff is
rubbish. No one knows what the
future holds.

YURI

I guess you are right, I didn't think
we would get this far, but we did...

*(Yuri pulls a card from a
Tarot deck, he gets the
'FOOL'.)*

...and my great aunt did fail to
predict a train would drive through
her house.

DMITRY

See, what did I tell you, it's all
rubbish. You just don't know what is
going to happen next...

*(The crowd begin screaming
and pointing towards London*

*and his group of ex-SAS
soldiers flailing around in
the collapsed balloon.
Suddenly, the basket falls
from the sky and London and
his men hit the ground hard.
Dmitry turns to see what the
commotion is and pushes Yuri
out of the way and dives on
the ground.)*

...Look out!

*(London and his men sail past
Yuri and Dmitry along with
the basket and collapsed
balloon and crash into the
stand. Yuri climbs out from
a carousel of Tarot cards and
gets to his feet.)*

                    YURI
What did you do that for?...

*(Dmitry stands back up and
points towards the basket and
wrecked display.)*

                    DMITRY
I was saving your life.

*(They both look at the mess
and the fallen balloon.)*

                    YURI
I am glad you were here, I didn't
even see it coming.

                   DMITRY
It was only crowd screaming that
alerted me.

                    YURI
All the same, it was quick thinking
on your part, thank you.

                   DMITRY
Funny thing though...

     *(Dmitry scratches his head
     and looks at the mess.)*

...I could have sworn one of the guys
clinging to the basket bore a
striking resemblance to that English
astronaut George London.

     (Yuri brushes himself down.)

                    YURI
I would imagine that is the last
person we would see riding in a
balloon in Moscow city.

                   DMITRY
I guess you are right.

     (Dmitry and Yuri look on as

*the stand collapses to the
floor and rails of ethnic
clothing and boxes of Tarot
cards spill out everywhere.
From within the Debris field
someone starts to move.)*

YURI
Someone is moving!

*(Carter pulls himself out of
the basket and falls to the
ground. From the inside of
his tunic, the Gold Medallion
of Life rolls out and stops
at Yuri's feet. Yuri bends
down and picks it up.)*

YURI
Look Dmitry, my medallion from the
monster ship.

*(He shows it to Dmitry.
Dmitry studies it with
interest.)*

DMITRY
You are right, but what is it doing
here and why does that chap have it?

CARTER
Oi, give that back.

(Dmitry and Yuri look towards

*Carter. Before long,
Pilkington, Winslow and
Cartwright start to emerge
from the inside of the
balloon.)*

DMITRY
Where did you get this?

CARTER
That's none of your bleeding
business. It's mine, now give it
back.

DMITRY
I am making it my business. This was
in our possession a couple of days
ago. I want to know how you got it.

*(Carter pulls out his knife.
Cavendish and London appear
from the back of the stand
dishevelled.)*

CARTER
Now, I've asked you to give that
bleedin' medallion back to me.

LONDON
Steady Carter, I'll take over from
here.

CARTER
But they've stolen the medallion.

		(Dmitry and Yuri look at
		George London.)

DMITRY
It is you. I thought I recognised
that greasy mop of yours. You snake,
I ought to kill you.

		(London looks on perplexed.)

LONDON
I'm afraid you chaps have me confused
with someone else.

DMITRY
Not likely. I never forget a face,
especially one that takes the only
escape pod and leaves Yuri and I to
die in space.

		(The blood drains from
		London's face.)

LONDON
Dmitry? Yuri? I didn't recognise
you.

DMITRY
It is true we are not looking our
best, but we have been through a lot.

                    LONDON
But you are dead?

                    YURI
Contrary to popular belief, we
survived our little jaunt in space.
No thanks to you.

                    CAVENDISH
London, who is this?

                    LONDON
This is the Russian cosmonauts Yuri
Chekov and Dmitry Usakov.

                    CAVENDISH
I thought they died a few days ago in
that I.S.S incident?

                    LONDON
So did I. How is this possible?

                    DMITRY
It would take rather a long time to
explain just now and we are still
trying to get our lives back. We
have already spent too much time in
your company and must get to the News
Station. Once the people know what
you have done, they will no doubt
come looking for you to answer some
difficult questions.

LONDON
What difficult questions?

YURI
Jumping into the escape pod with your
English pal and leaving the American
and us to die.

LONDON
We had no choice. I'd already
disarmed four of the bombs your
government had placed on the Space
Station. I was on my way to disarm
the fifth one when the thing blew up.
Poor old Wells and I barely made it
out with our lives. We thought you'd
been blown up. We tried to go back,
but once the flames came rushing
towards us, we had no alternative but
to leave.

YURI
You say you disarmed the bombs?

LONDON
Yes of course. Who else do you think
did it?

          (Yuri goes red in the face.
          Dmitry looks at Yuri with
          disdain.)

DMITRY
So, your mouse disabled bombs by

chewing through wire?

                    YURI
Well, it seemed only logical solution
at time.

                   LONDON
Wait. You thought your mouse had
chewed through the wires of the
bombs?...

     (London starts to laugh.)

...I say, that's a scream. How you
chaps made it back must be a riot.

     (London continues to laugh.)

                  DMITRY
We still have much to settle. You
told the press we were responsible
for the explosion on the Station.

     (London stops laughing.)

                   LONDON
Had to say something old boy. Could
hardly tell the press I worked for
MI5 and I was posing as an astronaut.
I knew your government was involved
in an operation to destroy the
Station, but I didn't know who the
players were. Didn't think for a
minute we'd only have a couple of

days to investigate.

                    DMITRY
The man you are looking for is
General Gerasimov, he is behind the
whole affair. He wants this
medallion...

        (Dmitry holds up the
        medallion.)

...The medallion has special powers,
something to do with eternal life.
We need to destroy it.

                    CARTER
Nobody's destroying nothing, that's
mine...

        (Carter goes to grab the
        medallion when shots ring out
        across the Square. Several
        shots bounce off the back of
        some tarot card boxes next to
        them and they dive for
        cover.)

                    LONDON
Take cover!

        (Everyone scrambles behind
        the boxes of tarot cards and
        shelving units. Shots
        continue to be fired. The

*parade stops and the Girl
Scouts run in all directions
screaming. Dmitry peers out
from behind a box.)*

DMITRY
Look Yuri, General Gerasimov and his
soldiers.

*(Dmitry takes out the laser
gun and fires it towards the
oncoming soldiers that are
moving amongst the crowds of
people.)*

YURI
That scumbag. Looks like we're for
it now.

LONDON
I take it this is someone you know?

DMITRY
Not by choice. He is the one I just
mentioned, General Gerasimov.

LONDON
The cad. Looks like an unsavoury
type to me.

YURI
Dmitry, what are we going to do?

DMITRY
We are pretty well pinned down here.
Not much cover if we move.

YURI
Dmitry, hold up the medallion, that's
what he wants.

CARTER
That's my medallion!

(Dmitry holds up the
medallion and we hear General
Gerasimov's voice.)

GENERAL GERASIMOV
Cease fire!

LONDON
That seems to have done the trick.

DMITRY
The General wants this medallion
pretty badly.

CARTER
Well he can't have it, it's mine.

LONDON
Do be quiet Carter. No one is
getting anything.

CAVENDISH
Maybe we should make a run for it
while they've stopped shooting.

DMITRY
The English love running away from a
problem. A true Russian faces a
problem head on.

CAVENDISH
Are you calling me yellow?

DMITRY
What is that expression Yuri the
English like to use.

YURI
Anyone for tennis?

DMITRY
No, not that one. The other one.

YURI
Oh, if the cap fits, wear it.

DMITRY
That is it.

CARTWRIGHT
I think we ought to leave while we
can. This is obviously an internal
problem. Both sides are Russian.

PILKINGTON
Winslow's already left.

LONDON
Winslow's left, I don't believe it.

PILKINGTON
See for yourself.

(London looks around for
Winslow and he appears to
have left.)

LONDON
Damn that Winslow fellow. Can't
believe he'd just up and go.

DMITRY
That is true colour of English.

LONDON
Listen Dmitry, I'm sorry for what
happened on the Space Station, but I
can assure you I'm not going anywhere
now, and that stands for all my men.

CAVENDISH
Pilkington and Cartwright have gone.

LONDON
This is mutiny of the tallest order.
They are all a bunch of mutineers.

                    CARTER
Don't you have to be on board a ship
to commit mutiny, I think you mean
desertion. They are all deserters,
that's what you mean.

                    LONDON
Yes, alright Carter. I'm glad you
paid attention at school, but it's
not helping matters.

                GENERAL GERASIMOV
Come out with your hands up. I only
want the medallion. Nobody else has
to get hurt.

                    YURI
What shall we do Dmitry?

                    DMITRY
Let me think a minute.

Scene fades.

ACT 6, SCENE 9

Outside the Red Neval, KAL pulls a wooden spoon and part of a saucepan from the stabilising blade and places it in a bag. He tightens some bolts and moves around to the crafts windscreen. He bangs on the glass to tell MacTavish to pull the lever.

MACTAVISH
Aye, just a minute. I forgotten what one I need to pull...

(Outside the window KAL is pointing to a lever with a blue knob.)

... Aye, laddie. Keep your locks on, I'm doing it!

(MacTavish pulls the lever with the blue knob.)

COMPUTER'S VOICE
Reinitialising horizontal stabilisers. Stabilisers are engaged. Two minutes before normal time begins.

(KAL walks back into the bridge.)

                    MACTAVISH
Looks like you fixed the kink, fit
was wrong?

         (KAL takes out a wooden spoon
         and part of a saucepan from
         his bag.)

                      KAL
I found these objects stuck in the
stabilisers. Some sort of space junk
by the looks of it.

                 COMPUTER'S VOICE
Normal time commencing in 10 seconds.

                      KAL
Better get ready. Going to have to
pump the brakes hard if we don't want
to crash...

         (The ship resumes its course
         and speed. The Red Neval
         punches through the clouds
         and the city comes into view.
         They arrive a few minutes in
         the past.)

...Hold on. That's it, we're safe
now.

                    MACTAVISH
Good, I will jus' have a wee dram
tae calm my nerves.

                    KAL
Something's coming up on the scanner.
It would seem the Medallion of Life
is just up ahead.

          *(The Red Neval arrives at the
          Red Square a few minutes
          before Winslow disappears.
          On one of the computer
          screens, an overhead view of
          the city can be seen. KAL
          pushes a button, and the view
          changes and zooms into eight
          figures that are standing in
          the centre of a collapsed
          stand. A downed hot air
          balloon is also at their
          location. The men seem to be
          engaged in a heated
          discussion.)*

                 MACTAVISH
Have you found it?

                    KAL
Yes, but I can't seem to pinpoint
it's exact location. One of these
Earthlings has it, but the computer
is having trouble choosing which one.

                 MACTAVISH
Why dinnae ye just grab the lot and
we can search them one by one.

                    KAL
That's not a bad idea. We can use
the grappler and put them straight
into individual confinement cells and
search them one by one.

                 MACTAVISH
Great, who shall we start with?

                    KAL
Let's take the small one at the back
of the group and then grab the next
two and work our way forward. Seems
to be some sort of weaponry being
fired. Deploying grappler...

        *(A rope with a hook descends
        from the Red Neval and snares
        Winslow. He is lifted up in
        the air and straight into a
        holding cell. The grappler
        is deployed again and
        Cartwright and Pilkington are
        taken.)*

...Going to be a bit tricky grabbing
the remaining group, they are all
crouched down amongst those boxes.
Looks like the Medallion is still in
the group.

        *(The grappler is deployed
        again and Carter, London and
        Cavendish are taken. Dmitry
        and Yuri stand up to*

*negotiate with General
Gerasimov and Dmitry looks
back to talk to London.)*

                    DMITRY
Look Yuri, they have all scarpered.
They are all chicken. Can't believe
that guy has run off again. What a
scumbag.

                    YURI
I never liked that guy, and he was
obviously lying about the bombs.
Doris saved us not him.

               GENERAL GERASIMOV
Good.   Now walk towards us.

        *(On board the Red Neval,
        Winslow, Pilkington,
        Cartwright, Cavendish, Carter
        and London are individually
        encased in glass tubes 8ft
        high by 3ft wide. KAL is now
        locking on to Dmitry and
        Yuri.)*

                     KAL
The Medallion is still down there.
It must be one of these two guys.
They have moved away from the boxes,
I can grab them now.

        (The Grappler is deployed

*again and Dmitry and Yuri are
pulled high into the air.)*

                    YURI
Dmitry, what is happppennnniinnggg!

            *(Dmitry and Yuri enter the
            Red Neval and are instantly
            encased in their own glass
            prison next to the others.)*

                    DMITRY
Trapped again. This is getting to be
an annoyance. Look, the English are
here too.

                    YURI
At least they didn't run off like we
thought.

                    DMITRY
That is another annoyance. I like to
think badly of them. It gives life a
purpose.

            *(On the bridge of the Red
            Neval, KAL activates the
            hover mode and switches to
            autopilot. He walks over to
            a language capturing device
            and puts it in his pocket.)*

                    KAL
MacTavish, I think we should go and
see our new visitors.

                 MACTAVISH
Aye, I have always liked the zoo.

                    KAL
They're not animals MacTavish, they
are intelligent life forms.

                 MACTAVISH
Aye, I ken that.

        (KAL and MacTavish enter a
        large white room where 30
        glass cylinders are in a
        parallel formation 2ft apart.
        15 glass tubes fixed to the
        floor face another 15 on the
        other side. A space of 8ft
        separates them in the middle.
        In eight of the tubes are the
        Earthlings: London,
        Cavendish, Pilkington,
        Carter, Winslow, Cartwright,
        Dmitry and Yuri. Winslow,
        Cartwright and Pilkington are
        unconscious and the others
        are all shouting at one
        another. No audible
        conversation can be heard.
        They instantly go quiet when
        KAL and MacTavish walk up to

the tubes.)

MACTAVISH

Odd looking bunch. A bitty like an
Állir-rog, but they died out years
ago.

KAL

Yes, I suppose they are...

*(KAL takes out his language
capturing device and holds it
towards Carter. Carter moves
closer to the glass.)*

...Now, we just need them to say a
few words and I will understand their
language.

CARTER

Let us out of here you pale faced
freak. You and that turban wearing
boggled eyed Morlock are for it big
time.

LONDON

Carter, calm down. They haven't done
anything to harm us yet. Let's just
try and work out what they want...

*(London is opposite Dmitry
and Yuri. He looks at
Dmitry. Yuri and Dmitry look
concerned.)*

...Dmitry, do you have any idea
what's going on here? Have you seen
these creatures before?

                    DMITRY
Yes.

                    LONDON
Well, Maybe you could enlighten us?

                    DMITRY
The white fellow is bad news. We met
and killed his psychotic sister a
couple of days ago. The turban
headed fellow is from a planet far
away. He probably wants to know what
happened to the Monster ship that
powered the dome. At this early
stage of introduction, I believe
ignorance is best.

        (London looks at his men.)

                    LONDON
Looks like we're a bit out of our
league here chaps. It would seem
Dmitry and Yuri have a better handle
on the situation. Perhaps we should
let them handle it.

                    CARTER
What? They've still got my
medallion.

LONDON
Do shut up Carter.

                    (*KAL begins to receive
                    information from the Language
                    capturing device.*)

                         KAL
Uploading... Data file transfer...
Uploading... Upload complete.

                    MACTAVISH
Does that mean you can ken them?

                         KAL
Yes, I can understand them.

                    MACTAVISH
They sound like a bunch of StorrÁps
having a squawk to me.

                         KAL
Yes, well, let's ask them a question.
This one seems quite docile. I think
I'll start with him...

          (*KAL walks over to Winslow.*)

...We are from a-no-ther plan-et. We
mean you no harm. We are look-ing
for an ob-ject, The Me-dal-lion of
Life. Have you seen it?

          (*Winslow is curled up in a*

*ball and is starting to wake
up. He is sweating
profusely. He leans forward
and throws up a lot of food.
Ham, cheese, bread, napkins,
paper plates, tomatoes,
olives and anchovies spill
out onto the floor in various
states of mastication.)*

CAVENDISH
Leave him be. He's sick.

*(London taps the glass to
attract KAL and MacTavish.
They look over to him. He
motions them closer.)*

LONDON
That's right. Winslow has a virus.
He has the plague. If I was you I
would let us go before you catch it.
The plague's not to be trifled with.
Bad for the complexion.

MACTAVISH
Fit are they saying, it hurts ma
lugs!

KAL
They are saying that this Earthling
has a contagious disease and that it
would be best if we let them go
before we get contaminated.

                    MACTAVISH
Disease? I dinnae like diseases,
especially animal ones. Best to burn
them, it's the only way to destroy it
for sure.

          (Dmitry looks over towards
          London.)

                    DMITRY
Shut up English. What do you think
they are going to do if you tell them
we have plague?

                    LONDON
I was hoping they would let us go.

                    DMITRY
They will kill us all.

          (KAL walks over to Dmitry.)

                    KAL
Your friend? Is sick, yes?

          (KAL points at Winslow.)

                    DMITRY
No. Travel to ship was too fast. He
has brought up lunch.

                    MACTAVISH
Fit's goin' on, we should burn the

lot of them?

                    KAL
It's alright MacTavish. It's just a
stomach upset.

                 MACTAVISH
Well, that's alright. I get that all
the time when I've had a drink.

     (KAL continues to talk to
     Dmitry.)

                    KAL
We are look-ing for a gold me-dal-
lion. We know one of you have it,
but we don't know which one?

     (Carter pushes his face
     against the glass.)

                  CARTER
Say a word and I'll cut your throat
out.

                 DMITRY
A medallion?

                    KAL
Yes. It is round with se-ver-al pre-
ci-ous stones.

                    YURI
Why does everybody want that
medallion, I wish I had never found
it. We have had nothing but bad luck
since I stole it from that dead
Captain. It is a big lesson learned
Dmitry. Never steal from a dead
alien.

     (KAL looks at Dmitry.)

                    KAL
So, you have the Me-dal-lion?

                    YURI
Who me? No, I don't have it!

                    KAL
Then who does?

                    YURI
Will you let us go if I tell you who
has the medallion?

                    KAL
Yes.

          (At that moment, the ship
          begins to shake violently and
          everyone falls to the floor.
          Alarms sound out and a big
          explosion is heard.)

MACTAVISH
Fit's going on?

KAL
I think we are under attack. We
better get to the bridge.

> *(KAL and MacTavish leave the
> white room and head for the
> bridge. Another explosion
> occurs and the glass tubes
> begin to crack. Carter hits
> his tube with his knife and
> the cylinder breaks and he is
> free. The ship begins to
> groan and suddenly starts to
> fall. The hull starts to
> crack and the side of the
> ship falls off revealing the
> clouds and the sky.)*

YURI
Dmitry, we are falling.

DMITRY
Hold on to something Yuri.

YURI
There is nothing to hold on to.

LONDON
Carter? There is a lever with a blue
knob on it; over there, by the wall.
I think it's the release for these

tubes. Go and pull it...

(*The Red Neval groans and
complains and whining noises
fill the air. Wind whips in
from the outside and sounds
of engines failing and metal
grinding reverberate the
white room. Carter pulls the
lever and the glass cylinders
retract into the floor.*)

...That's it carter, well done.

                    CAVENDISH
Quick, over there. Another room...

(*A large storage cupboard
leading off of the white room
is seen in the corner. It is
full of blankets and
bedding.*)

...We might be safe in there. Quick,
get in!

(*The Red Neval picks up speed
and an engine explodes.
Flames envelope the exterior
of the ship and it goes into
freefall. KAL and MacTavish
get to the bridge and it's on
fire.*)

                    KAL
Quick MacTavish, hit the time delay
button.

          *(MacTavish runs forward and
          hits the time delay button.
          The board spins round and
          stops.)*

            COMPUTER'S VOICE
Time delay activated, you have 45
seconds.

                    KAL
45 seconds?

                 MACTAVISH
45 seconds, I cannae do anything in
45 seconds. It takes me longer than
that to find a corkscrew.

                    KAL
There must be something we can do?

Scene fades.

ACT 6, SCENE 10

1.24pm. Saturday 18th October, 2025, The Red Square, Moscow, Russia. General Gerasimov has been firing at the Red Neval spaceship for the past two minutes and has mobilised his ground troops into strategic positions. High in the clouds, the Red Neval has suffered major damage and is hurtling towards Earth at breakneck speed. Debris falls from the sky and explodes on the ground breaking shop windows and setting off car alarms. Crowds of people gather round to look at the fireball in the sky and watch the spectacle in awe. Channel 5 News is on the scene setting up to film the action and Anastasia Bedlumvich is preparing herself to go live. She fixes her hair and the seam of her stockings and looks into the camera. She is holding a microphone and starts to test for voice levels. She looks at the cameraman and He counts her in with his fingers.

ANASTASIA BEDLUMVICH
...For the past 2 minutes, the
Russian army, under the charge of
General Gerasimov, have been firing
on an unknown vessel in the sky. The
vessel is like nothing we have seen
before and is believed to be of
extraterrestrial origin. Although

the vessel has shown no signs of hostile intent, it is believed to be of a significant threat to the security of our nation. Over the past minute, the alien vessel has sustained considerable damage from army artillery and has lost what looks like two of its engines. There have been several explosions and the vessel seems to be on fire. As you can see, it's sheer pandemonium here and the annual Autumn Festival has been ruined. Tanks and heavy artillery are continuing to fire at the vessel and people are running everywhere to find shelter and safety. There now seems to be a real concern as to whom these invaders might be and what their intentions are. That is the billion ruble question on everyone's lips. Up until 20 seconds ago the alien craft was breaking up and beginning to fall from the sky. Now, it seems to be suspended in time like a film on pause. As you know, over the last 2 days Moscow has seen its fair share of problems with two terrorist bombings and a bizarre meteor shower. It was only this morning that city officials gave the go ahead for the autumn festival due to concerns about the level of black dust in the air...

(Inside the Red Neval, KAL

deploys the emergency breaking system and detaches the cargo bay, the swimming pool and the horticultural room to reduce weight and speed. The vessel returns to normal space and large sections of the ship fall away. It begins to slow down but it is going to crash.)

...Wait, it's moving again. It's heading straight for the Russian army...

(Anastasia Bedlumvich dives to the floor as the Red Neval plunges into the Red Square. Tanks and military vehicles are tossed into the air as the vessel slides along the ground throwing everything out and up. General Gerasimov and his men are swallowed up by a sea of concrete and metal. Scraping and grinding noises are heard and explosions burst out like spots from a teenagers face and the whole city shakes. After 37 terrible seconds, the Red Neval comes to a stop. Anastasia Bedlumvich gets to her feet and her cameraman starts to film

again.)

...As you can see, the alien vessel has crashed in Red Square killing all of the Russian army along with General Gerasimov. The alien vessel has sustained major damage and I can't imagine any of the occupants will have survived...

> *(From the wreck of the Red Neval, the dust begins to clear and two figures start to emerge from within. From out of a hole in the side of the ship they come into view.)*

...Wait, something is coming out of the ship...

> *(Crowds of people start to return to the square to look at the vessel. Dmitry and Yuri scramble amongst the wreck and fall to the ground. They are covered with dust and look filthy.)*

...It is people. The alien's are like us. This could be the end of our civilisation as we know it...

> *(Dmitry and Yuri walk over to Anastasia Bedlumvich. They*

are very dirty.)

...Two of the creatures are walking over to me. This could be first contact.

                    DMITRY
Finally. I can't believe the stuff a guy has to go through to get on the News these day...

        (Dmitry snatches the
        microphone from Anastasia
        Bedlumvich.)

...I am Dmitry Usakov...

        (Dmitry puts his arm around
        Yuri and looks at the
        camera.)

...And this is my good friend Yuri Chekov...

             ANASTASIA BEDLUMVICH
It's the dead cosmonauts. They've taken on human form. Run for your life!

        (Anastasia Bedlumvich runs
        away screaming, but the
        cameraman keeps filming.)

                         DMITRY
Contrary to popular belief, we did
not die on International Space
Station and we have not been taken
over by alien life form. My friend
and I have survived an incredible
ordeal and have returned to Earth to
let you know the terrible secrets the
government have been keeping from
you...

          *(Crowds of people gather
          round to hear Dmitry's
          words.)*

...Our world is flat and we have been
trapped on it for 5,000 years by an
invisible dome powered by an alien
ship.

          *(The crowd of people start to
          chuckle.)*

                         YURI
We have proof...

          *(Yuri pulls out his little
          tartan bear and holds it up.)*

...Inside this bear we have evidence
to prove it...

          (The crowd start to laugh.)

CROWD MEMBER
It must be fake. They must be
shooting a movie. They don't even
look like the Russian cosmonauts Yuri
Chekov and Dmitry Usakov. They are
always so clean and smart. I can't
imagine they would wear those
clothes.

DMITRY
But we have been through a lot. This
is crazy, how do you explain alien
vessel behind us?

ANOTHER CROWD MEMBER
Special effects?

DMITRY
But you are here. You have seen it
with your own eyes.

(*Fires spread throughout the
alien vessel and bangs and
pops fire off like
fireworks.*)

THIRD CROWD MEMBER
It's amazing what they can do these
days with plastic models and bits of
cardboard...

(*A shot rings out across the
square and the third crowd
member falls to the floor*

clutching his chest.)

...I've been shot.

*(The third crowd member dies.
A forth crowd member bends
down to look at the body and
gets blood on his hands.)*

                    FORTH CROWD MEMBER
It's real. They really are aliens.
They're doppelgangers. They'll kill
us all. Run for your life!

*(The crowd disperses quickly
and only Dmitry, Yuri and the
cameraman remain. A lone
figure walks across the
square holding an AK-47.)*

                         DMITRY
What is the point, they are all
morons Yuri...

*(Dmitry throws the microphone
on the dead man's chest and
Yuri and Dmitry crouch down
behind a concrete planter.
Another shot rings out and
the cameraman falls to the
ground. He is dead. Dmitry
and Yuri peer over the
planter to see the
approaching man. He comes
into view. The man has three*

*fingers on his left hand and
he has a burnt face.)*

...Now, who is this guy. We have
enough trouble without another
lunatic in our lives.

                    YURI
I think it is that Vadim guy.

                    DMITRY
Who?

                    YURI
The son of the father whose identity
I stole. The one who planted bomb on
Space Station.

                    DMITRY
What! How did he get here? This day
keeps on getting worse.

          *(Bullets ring out across the
          top of the planter and Dmitry
          and Yuri crouch down.)*

               VADIM SCHEKOV
Come out. I promise I will make it
quick.

                    YURI
Dmitry, do you still have the laser
gun?

                    DMITRY
          Yes, it is in my...

                     YURI
          What is it?

                    DMITRY
          I must have dropped it.

                 VADIM SCHEKOV
          Come out of there. I promise I will
          kill you quick. There is no shame in
          death. It is a great release.

               (Dmitry shouts out.)

                    DMITRY
          If you feel that way about it, why
          don't you kill yourself.

                 VADIM SCHEKOV
          Sometimes it has crossed my mind, but
          today is not one of those days.
          Today I get to avenge my father's
          death and the man that took his life.

                     YURI
          I did not take your father's life.
          He choked on fish bone. If you have
          complaint with someone, it should be
          the Russian Railway Company, it is
          their fault. They have been serving
          up inferior food products for last 30

years. They are ones to blame for
your father's death. It is the chef
you should kill. The one who
prepared fish. You could also blame
college where he learnt his knife
skills. It just goes to show that
poor training can cost lives.

DMITRY
What about the Chef's parents?

YURI
That is right Dmitry, they did not
teach him well.

VADIM
Quiet. I will take your suggestions
under advisement, meanwhile, I wish
to execute my plan. Stand up. Don't
make me come and get you.

*(KAL and MacTavish stumble
from the bridge section of
the ship and fall to the
ground. A loud banging is
heard and London, Cavendish,
Winslow, Cartwright, Carter
and Pilkington exit the alien
vessel and collapse on the
ground. They look battered
and bruised, but alive.
Crowds of people carrying
clubs, knives, cricket bats,
rocks and pitch forks walk*

*back to the square to see
what is happening. The Red
Neval is now a fireball and
smoke pours into the sky.)*

MACTAVISH
I guess we are going to be here for a
while?

KAL
Yes, I don't think we can patch the
Red Neval back together. She has
made her one and only voyage.

*(Vadim walks closer to the
concrete planter.)*

VADIM SCHEKOV
Now, come out of there!

*(Dmitry and Yuri get to their
feet and walk around the
planter to face Vadim.
London and his group of ex-
SAS soldiers look on from
there position to see what is
happening.)*

DMITRY
Goodbye old friend, it was nice
knowing you.

*(Vadim raises his AK-47 and
goes to fire when a knife*

*enters his neck. Carter
walks over to Vadim and pulls
the knife out of his neck and
then turns to Dmitry.)*

                    CARTER
Now, give me back my bleedin'
medallion?

          *(KAL and MacTavish get to
          their feet and walk over to
          London and his men. From
          around the corner Miss
          Decapinovsky and an angry
          group of women enter The
          Square and notice the strange
          looking creatures from
          another planet.)*

               MISS DECAPINOVSKY
There they are! Demons! Goblins!
Kill them all!

          *(A crowd of women armed with
          flagpoles and sticks join the
          already angry mob. They
          start to run towards Dmitry,
          Yuri, KAL, MacTavish, London
          and his gang of ex-SAS
          soldiers.)*

                    DMITRY
Yuri, Run! They are all mad...

*(The group of ten fugitives
run down the street and enter
an alley where the shops
consist of fashion wear -
dresses, shoes, hats,
jewellery and cosmetics.
They run past a dress shop
where the window is broken
and climb inside. They hide
behind a counter as the angry
mob run by.)*

...That was close. I think we better
stay here for a while.

                    CARTER
Now, hand over that medallion.

                    DMITRY
Here, have the thing. It is nothing
but trouble.

          *(Dmitry hands over the
          medallion to Carter.)*

                    CARTER
Thanks!

                    MACTAVISH
Is that the Medallion of lee?

                    KAL
It certainly looks like it, but it's
of no use to us now. The mission's

over.

> *(In the back of the shop a*
> *voice can be heard singing 'I*
> *will survive' by Gloria*
> *Gaynor and a figure emerges*
> *from the dressing room*
> *wearing a bright orange*
> *dress, orange tights, orange*
> *shoes, orange hat, orange*
> *gauntlet gloves, orange*
> *handbag and a string of white*
> *pearls.)*

DMITRY
It is you. Why are you here, I
thought I told you to go home?

MOON MAN
I couldn't go home dressed like that,
in all those filthy rags, what would
my poor mother say?

LONDON
Do you know this person Dmitry?

DMITRY
Yes, we are old friends.

YURI
Dmitry, what are we going to do now?

> *(Dmitry looks around the shop*
> *at all the women's fashion*

hanging on the rails.)

                    DMITRY
Let me think a minute.

Scene fades.

            End of Part III

        FIND OUT WHAT HAPPENS NEXT IN:

UPRISING - PART ONE

If you enjoyed this book and would
like to be notified of my next
release, please subscribe to the
News, Events and Much more section of
my website under the 'Contact'
heading. If you have time, please
rate and leave a review on Amazon to
help increase awareness of this
series. Many Thanks, Sam Lucas.

To see the complete collection of books in this series,
please go to: **www.samlucasbooks.com**